Endii

ENDINGS

by *'Abd al-Rahman Munif*
translated by Roger Allen

Interlink Books

An imprint of Interlink Publishing Group, Inc.
Northampton, Massachusetts

To the memory of Janet Lee Stevens, who first introduced me to this work.
—R.A.

First paperback edition published in 2007 by

INTERLINK BOOKS
An imprint of Interlink Publishing Group, Inc.
46 Crosby Street, Northampton, Massachusetts 01060
www.interlinkbooks.com

Published in Arabic as *al-Nihayat*, 1977. First published in the English
language by Quartet Books Ltd 1988

ISBN 1-56656-669-X
ISBN 13: 978-1-56656-669-8

Printed and bound in the United States of America
10 9 8 7 6 5 4 3 2 1

Translator's Introduction

The novel is a literary genre which throughout its history has taken as one of its primary topics the nature of modernity and the process of change. Bearing in mind the rapidity of its development in the post-industrial era, it should not surprise us that authors of this genre have focused their attention on the problems of the emerging middle class and, in particular, the life of the modern city. Perhaps one might suggest that novels have been and are written in the main by city dwellers about city dwellers for city dwellers, thus covering the author–text–reader triad favoured by much contemporary narratology. Novels set in the countryside are by comparison a rarer commodity, and particularly within the context of the Arabic novel. Novels set entirely in the desert are, I would suggest, almost unheard of; and therein lies the uniqueness of *Endings* by 'Abd al-Rahman Munif.

While the corpus of Arabic novels available in English translation is continually growing, it remains small by comparison with other world literature traditions. Furthermore the list has certain characteristics: the majority of novels are written by Egyptians, and they are set among the middle-class population in the capital cities of the Middle East. Both these features are, I hasten to add, a fair reflection of the tradition itself. By contrast, *Endings* is by a Saudi novelist; this may indeed be the first translation of a Saudi novel. 'Abd al-Rahman Munif was born in 1933. He has studied in Yugoslavia and France and holds a doctorate degree in petroleum economics. He currently lives in Boulogne on the Channel coast. For a time he lived in Iraq where he became a close colleague and friend of the great Palestinian *littérateur,* Jabra Ibrahim Jabra, who lives in Baghdad. Munif was editor of the petroleum journal, *Al-Naft wa al-Tanmiya* (Petroleum and Development). For some years now he has devoted himself exclusively to creative writing, and, as I write these words, he is in the process of finishing the third volume of his huge trilogy, *Mudun al-Milh* (Cities of Salt).

Munif's works in order of publication are: *Al-Ashjar wa-ghtiyal Marzuq* (The Trees and Marzuq's Assassination, 1973), *'Indama tarakna al-Jisr* (When We Abandoned the Bridge, 1976), *Sharq al-Mutawassit* (East of the Mediterranean, 1977), *Qissat Hubb Majusiyya* (Gypsy Love Story, n.d.), *Al-Nihayat* (Endings, 1978), *Sibaq al-Masafat al-Tawila* (Long Distance Race, 1979) and *Mudun al-Milh* (Cities of Salt), a trilogy of which two volumes have been published thus far: *Al-Tih* (The Wilderness, 1984) and *Al-Ukhdud* (The Trench, 1985). The third volume is to be called *Taqasim al-Layl wa al- Nahar* (Divisions of Night and Day). As if this enormous outburst of creative activity were not sufficient, Munif also embarked with his friend, Jabra Ibrahim Jabra, on the fascinating project of writing a novel together; *'Alam bila Khara'it* (Mapless World, 1982) is the result of this cooperative effort.

Munif's themes in these works vary a great deal. Thus *Sharq al-Mutawassit* is an unnervingly graphic portrayal of the techniques used by the state somewhere 'east of the Mediterranean' (otherwise unspecified) to control the activities of its citizenry, whether in the prisons of the country itself or while studying in Europe. *Sibaq al-Masafat al-Tawila* places its characters into the political situation in Iran at the time of the Prime Ministership of Mossadeg. *Mudun al-Milh* represents the author's return to a consideration of the political and social circumstances in his own homeland of Saudi Arabia. The work establishes a particular village and hero within the traditional desert society of Arabia and then uses them as a foil for the savage encroachment of oil interests on both the environment and its inhabitants. When completed, this trilogy will represent a fictional and, no doubt, continually critical assessment of the impact of the oil boom on traditional Saudi society. Here the professional training and creative instincts of Munif are combined in a most fertile way.

The one major aspect which sets *Endings* apart from most other novels is the role which place plays in the structuring and impact of the entire work. The environment impinges on almost every chapter, and no more so than in the striking opening to the novel:

> Drought. Drought again!
> When drought seasons come, things begin to change. Life and objects change. Humans change too, and no more so than in their moods! Deep down, melancholy feelings take root. They may seem fairly unobtrusive at first. But people will often get angry. When that happens, these feelings burst out into the open, assertive and unruly.

Droughts can, of course, occur anywhere in the world, but it is not long before the reader of *Endings* discovers that this drought is not merely some periodic statistic of meteorology, but an enduring condition faced by a community, the village of al-Tiba. Nowhere in the novel do we discover exactly where this village is on the map of the Arab world, and indeed a singular lack of both geographical specifics and chronology is one of the work's primary features. Al-Tiba thus becomes a symbol for any and all villages of its type, a paradigm for communities facing the wrath of nature unaided by modern technology. One of the clear implications of the events of this work is that, while the distant and alien city is glad to exploit the traditional hospitality of the village, it has yet to provide the struggling community with the means to battle the extreme forces of nature. Hence the import of the work's final pages. The descriptions of nature in this novel provide some of its most striking moments; Munif writes about the environs of the village, the hunting of animals, and above all, the fearsome sandstorm leading to the climax of the work, with a vividness and attention to detail which makes the location almost tangible.

The cruel vicissitudes of nature, the search for water and food, the imminence of danger and even death, these are all clearly depicted for the reader of *Endings*. As themes in works of Arabic literature they also have a history stretching back to the very beginnings of the tradition. The village of al-Tiba is right on the edge of the desert; it is, to use an anthropological term, 'liminal'. This same liminality is to be found as a contributing thematic element in the corpus of Arabic tribal poetry which was composed and performed in the period before the advent of Islam in the seventh century. The environment is the same, and so are the concerns of 'people'. One of the primary similes whereby the pre-Islamic poet expresses his particular vision is through descriptions of animals, and that very same feature is abundantly present in Munif's novel as well. This is found most notably in the series of stories which accompany 'Assaf's wake, but the descriptions of his dog and of the variety of birds and other creatures which share the harsh life of the community also contribute to the unusual atmosphere conveyed by the work. As 'the people of al-Tiba', that group which is invoked as an entity throughout *Endings*, discuss and argue about their past, present and future, and the forces of change, both natural and man-made, the reader is presented with a contemporary celebration of many of the traditional values which have survived the passage of time and the events of history, at least up till now.

This opening passage then sets the scene in a most effective and economical manner. But the reference to 'people' and 'humans' also establishes another feature of the narrative which is to pervade the novel. We have already observed the lack of references to *particular* place and time, something which lends an almost mythic aspect to the story. There is also the question of characters, or, in this case, a lack of them in the normally accepted sense. *Endings* is in fact singularly economical in its use of names of any kind. To be sure, we hear of Abu Zaku, the village carpenter, of the Mukhtar, and, above all, of 'Assaf. However, there is almost no concern with the portrayal of individual characters, whether through dialogue or description. Time and again throughout this work the narrative returns to the public voice of the storyteller as the reader is informed of yet another facet of 'the people of al-Tiba' and the usually forceful opinions of its older inhabitants. Indeed one of the most remarkable aspects of this novel is the length of time it takes to penetrate from the almost anthropological detail of the initial chapters to a more particular level of both events and people.

When all these features are combined with the narrative approach adopted by the 'speaker', the reader gets the impression that he or she is participating in something resembling a piece of contemporary folklore. The narrator is continually providing different possibilities to explain the phenomena described and presenting a variety of points of view on an item of contention (and the narrator provides descriptions of many of them). On some occasions the narrator will suggest that one of the versions is more plausible than the others, but the very process of incorporating into each episode a number of differing aspects and perspectives draws the reader into the narrative in a creative way. Indeed it becomes an imitation of the very process which it is describing: 'The people in al-Tiba know how to turn a story in that incredible way which makes everything seem to be of primary importance. This talent is passed on from father to son.' The narrator is obviously intimately acquainted with al-Tiba and its people, but he uses the narrative mode of limited omniscience to convey to the reader the way in which the capricious whims of nature are reflected in the attitudes, arguments and actions of the members of this community. Within this process, none of the usual cues is provided for the reader. There are no chapter headings or numbers. As the wake over 'Assaf's body commences, we are informed within the narrative that a series of stories is to be told. However, the identity of each narrator is not provided, nor are beginnings and endings of the stories indicated in any particular way; in this translation I have provided a numerical sequencing for the stories myself. At the conclusion of the final story, the narrative continues without further ado. The effect of this narrative process is, I would suggest, very similar to that of participating in the creation and re-creation of a mythic tale, a process which has been described as 'expressing and therefore ... implicitly symbolizing certain deep-lying aspects of human and transhuman existence'. The narrator subtly invites the reader to listen as the traditions of the culture are tested to their limit and beyond.

It is a pleasure to acknowledge that this translation has been undertaken in consultation with the author. I would like to extend to him my most profound thanks for his encouragement. I have made every effort to convey in the English translation the clarity and neatness of his style, ranging from the gnomic pronouncements about the community as a whole to the highly poetic descriptions of nature and animals, to the narrative styles of the collection of stories (including extracts from the works of the great ninth-century polymath, al-Jahiz), to the liveliest of arguments and discussions. I can only hope that, after this attempt to transfer these various facets of the original into English, other readers will share my admiration for this unique contribution to contemporary fiction.

Endings

Drought. Drought again!

When drought seasons come, things begin to change. Life and objects change. Humans change too, and no more so than in their moods! Deep down, melancholy feelings take root. They may seem fairly unobtrusive at first. But people will often get angry. When that happens, these feelings burst out into the open, assertive and unruly. They can appear in a number of guises. As clouds scurry past high in the sky, people look up with angry, defiant expressions. With the arrival of drought, no home is left unscathed. Everybody bears some kind of mental or physical scar.

During the course of their long lives the old people have witnessed many gruesome periods. As a result, they have long since become inured to years of fatigue and the pangs of hunger. Even so, the very thought of drought seasons can still fill them with forebodings. They are the only ones who face the prospect with such resolution. At first people persevere doggedly and manage to put aside small amounts of grain so as to provide some form of sustenance during times of drought. But these small stockpiles soon run out or simply dwindle away. It is the same with spring water and the stream. At this point a frantic search for daily bread gets underway; in the process anxieties and premonitions start rearing their ugly heads and turn into horrible spectres. The phenomenon can be seen in any number of different guises: expressions on children's faces; the glum looks displayed by the men and the curses they use; and the tears which women shed for no apparent reason.

Yes, drought is back again. Here it comes, pushing a whole

host of things ahead of it. No one can explain how these things coincide or happen to be there at all. Take peasants, for example. They would bring baskets of eggs to the edge of town; sometimes they would even venture into the centre where the markets are crowded with people. Then there were shepherds whose entire annual income would be based on the sale of a few lambs. They used to bring in their flocks at the beginning of spring carrying the tiny, newborn lambs on their chests to sell in town. And then there were the crafty vendors who would bring in grapes, figs and apples on their pack animals. They used to weigh things out on primitive scales with sets of weights made out of pieces of polished stone; at first they would always overcharge people for their wares. But when these people came into town during a drought season, they would all look strangely different. Their clothing would be torn and have an odd colouring. They used to look anxious and sad. The powerful voices they would normally use to advertise their wares seemed by now to have slithered back down their throats; in their place all you heard were garbled sounds. Sometimes the town shopkeepers would ply them with terse, abrupt questions. The vendors from outside the town would have to repeat what they had been saying. But it was not the vendors' faces that these town shopkeepers were watching; what they had their eyes on were their hands or rather the tiny purses which the vendors kept firmly tied to the hems of whatever clothing they were wearing on their heads or bodies. When these people came into town during drought, they did not have any eggs, fruit, olives or lambs to sell. Instead they would try to purchase as much flour and sugar as their scant resources would permit. That applies even to shepherds, who were always particularly impetuous. They would demand such inflated prices for their lambs that, if it proved necessary, they preferred to bring their animals back to town a second time. Even if they did not buy or sell anything, they never seemed the slightest bit worried. However during years of drought like this one, they too become tentative and ingratiating. They are afraid their old and weak animals will die of hunger and thirst at any moment and are very anxious to get rid of them as quickly as possible.

There were still other salesmen who used to come into town at different times of year, bringing whatever produce was in season at the time. Sometimes they would simply come to take a look around. When drought came, these people would not bring anything at all. They would look for all the world like a group of hedgehogs that had rolled themselves up into balls and buried everything underground.

If these were only the surface manifestations of the total situation, then no one would be particularly surprised. After all, the relationship between the town and its environs is a powerful and continuing one. When changes start occurring, no one can afford to make snap judgements. As it was, odd things did start happening. For example, merchants who had normally been willing to make small loans to peasants and accept repayment during the harvest season (with a generous amount of interest added on, of course) now began to adopt a new procedure. Initially at least this procedure seemed fraught with all kinds of stipulations and was accompanied by not a little reluctance on the merchants' part. Before long they stopped making loans altogether, maintaining, of course, that such regrettable decisions were occasioned by a variety of disputes and other factors. Those few money-lenders who were still willing to offer some kind of financial assistance refused point-blank to postpone repayment until the following season. They insisted on new terms: peasants were required to sign over large segments of the land they owned to the money-lenders and their sons. These money-lenders did make a token effort to show good will. In the process they made use of the entire repertoire of platitudes which creditors can always be relied on to produce on such occasions. Here is a small example: 'This world of ours is a matter of life and death. Man cannot even guarantee that he will still be alive at the end of the very day he is living. So how can he possibly make any arrangements for his children's lives once he is dead and gone?' Nor was that all. They went on to say things like: 'As God Almighty says in the Holy Quran: "When you contract a debt upon one another for a stated term, write it down, and let a writer write it down between you justly."' Some peasants countered this insistence on the part of the money-lenders with an even more stubborn attitude. Initially at least they refused to have their land registered in this fashion. But before long they found themselves compelled to part with gold and silver heirlooms which had been collected and passed on through generations and to offer them as collateral for flour, sugar and a few yards of linen. Later on, some of them gave in and agreed to register their lands and orchards in accordance with the creditors' demands. But, with every deal that was signed, the prices for land in the village dropped, and that made the merchants even more reluctant to offer any help. They now refused to make any agreements which were not on their own terms and insisted that all the required procedures had to be carried out.

There are other things which come with drought. People are struck down by strange diseases, and death soon follows. Old people used to pass away out of sheer grief. With young people, it was distended stomachs at first, followed by jaundice and then total collapse. People became inured to the idea of death. It no longer managed to scare them as it usually did at other times, although it certainly did bring a number of sorrows and long-standing hatreds to the surface. When drought was at hand, a desperate premonition of impending disaster seemed to hover over every house and almost to burrow its insidious way into the bloodstream of every living creature. Even animals usually kept in paddocks or at the far end of orchards had an especially edgy and desperate look about them.

In years like this death and hunger were much in evidence and so were countless flocks of birds scurrying their way across the sky like so many fluffy clouds high in the heavens. They could be seen at all hours of the day and even in the dead of night. Without making the slightest sound they used to fly past high in the sky, almost as though they were heading for some far away and unfamiliar destination, maybe even death, without knowing either where it was or when they would get there. People would gaze forlornly at the birds, fondly wishing that they would fly closer to the ground or else come down for a short rest; then it might be possible to grab several of them and thus avoid the imminent threat of hunger. But, as it was, the birds continued their exhausting journey to some unknown destination. Everyone stared up at them with a sigh, waiting for something to happen, but nothing ever did. Flocks of geese, cranes and dozens of other types of birds could be seen as they flew past on their relentless migration. From time to time sand grouse started to appear too. Peasants had long since come to realize that this latter species only leaves its desert habitat and flies in towards pastured land when hunger and thirst have finally reduced its stamina and the various desert oases and water cisterns scattered around the place no longer contain a single drop of water. Obeying a natural instinct for survival these birds too started to abandon their normal cautious ways. Peasants noticed them heading for any place where they stood a chance of finding some crumbs to eat or a few drops of water.

They witnessed the same tragedy repeated right before their very eyes. Peasants were used to waiting patiently and even to displaying a certain conservatism born of a pessimistic outlook. If anyone questioned them about the various seasons and farming, they replied that seasons did not merely imply rainfall but a lot of other things as well. If the questioner persisted, they would summarize the whole situation as follows: 'Whatever God provides for us and the birds leave behind, that's what the seasons mean.' Deep down they are actually afraid of everything; that is why they make such statements. When no rainfall comes in the month when it is supposed to, they start worrying. If it comes early, crops start growing and show about an inch or two above the ground. When that happens, they worry in case the dry period will be followed by heavy rains; then the ground will get saturated, unwanted grass will grow, and everything will be spoiled. Even when the rain comes in reasonable amounts, spaced out evenly and at the right time, they still fuss till the end of May when it suddenly gets much hotter and everything burns to a crisp. At that point their hopes are dashed, and promises have to be broken. Men may have been promising their wives new clothes; the younger men in the community have reached the age of puberty and are eager to get married, always assuming that the new season will bring good tidings with it. All such promises have to be postponed, and all because the 'heatwave' (that is what they call it) has arrived and put an end to their fondest hopes.

No one likes to recall drought seasons ... When it is

particularly severe and keeps recurring year after year, most people prefer death or killing; they may even move away rather than have to face this prolonged agony of waiting. Others are driven to a level of vindictiveness and cruelty which people find hard to credit; indeed the perpetrators of such cruelty can hardly believe their own behaviour when they recall it later on and in different circumstances. For, if a man cannot vent his spleen on clouds and Him who sends them, then victims of another type have to be found. Husbands who normally show a great deal of tolerance and never swear or take a sudden swipe at anyone seem quite ready to abandon their normal behaviour without the slightest sense of remorse. At the least provocation they hit out and scream bloody murder over the most insignificant things. People who usually manage to put up a merry and optimistic front will be abruptly transformed into bitter scrooges, something which shows in both their attitude and behaviour. Even the most devout people who normally consider everything brought by the heavens as a test for mankind soon fall prey to these symptoms. In fact, they start swearing and blaspheming much worse than anyone else, to such an extent that people who have known them for ages wonder to themselves how such seemingly devout people can keep such a staggering lexicon of curses and wicked thoughts stored up inside them.

This then was the way most people behaved during that long, cruel year. Needless to say, every village and town in this microcosm had its own particular features and way of life: special names, cemeteries, drunkards, lunatics, rivers and streams to provide drinking water, and wedding seasons after the harvest. The village of al-Tiba was no different. It too had its own particular life-style, its graveyard and its weddings. It had its fair share of lunatics too, but they were not always in evidence. They had a special, crazy presence of their own. Sometimes they would seem big and strong; at others they could be utterly stupid and weird. But, in spite of everything, people sometimes managed to forget all about them. Al-Tiba also had its share of weddings, joys and sorrows too. More often than not, the weddings came after the harvest. When there was no rain and the ground became parched, the sad times came.

Wedding ceremonies might involve just a few people and for a specific period of time, but when years of drought came around, the gloomy expressions were everywhere to be seen, and the feeling persisted for a long time.

As is the case with villages throughout the world, al-Tiba has things of which it is proud. In other contexts these things may not seem particularly significant or important. But, as far as al-Tiba is concerned, they form a cross-section of those special features 'which set it apart from other hamlets and villages. They represent the result of the action of time and nature in all its cruelty, something which is not the case elsewhere. For example the inhabitants of other villages may have loud voices. Peasants will often have shrill, high-pitched voices. They talk a mile a minute and spice their chatter with proverbs and aphorisms. That is the way peasants are all over the place; it stems from sheer habit and the distances which separate people from each other in the fields, or else from the fact that they have to shout at some animals which go astray or others whose peculiar temperament takes them off to distant, unknown places; or it may even be due to the distance between houses and the gardens and orchards around them (in which a large variety of vegetables are grown). All these factors have combined to produce in the inhabitants of al-Tiba a particular kind of temperament. Many other factors could be cited as well. As a result, people in al-Tiba have a particular way of talking. Someone hearing them speak for the first time without being aware of the way they are and how they relate to each other might imagine they were squabbling or that a dispute had turned so nasty that something terrible was about to happen.

If this was all that was involved, it would not be terribly significant, particularly as far as it concerns peasants and those who understand their temperament. However these character-istics are accompanied by a special narrative technique which is the stock-in-trade of the people of al-Tiba. They will often meander away from the main topic and indulge in reminiscences. When they are telling stories culled from history, they milk the situation for all it is worth. If it were not for this trait, their special temperament would not be obvious at all, nor would the ever-present anxiety which characterizes everyone who lives in this village and others around it. Actually the trait may even reach as far as the city itself or at least some of its outer suburbs.

The people in al-Tiba know how to turn a story in that incredible way which makes everything seem to be of primary importance. This talent is passed on from father to son. As a result, in other people's eyes they come to seem special and even manage to persuade and exert some influence. This phenomenon cannot be explained away by suggesting that the whole thing is actually some kind of trickery or even flattery, or that it shows a malicious streak. It is quite simply a habit, and one that is subject to endless repetition.

There were those long nights when people would gather round and tell each other tales. These would go on and on. Challenges would be issued, and competitions would follow. All this would take place on summer and winter nights, in barns, alongside the village spring or clustered around braziers. The stories would all be fast-paced and effective, as close to a dream-world as one could imagine. People who were not good enough to participate in these story-telling sessions became totally different as soon as they found themselves among other people. They would retell the stories they had first heard in al-Tiba and embellish them with all the novel elements of fantasy their hearts desired. The resulting stories seemed so clever and skilful that they aroused as much admiration as envy.

Everyone who is born in al-Tiba, young or old, is a good listener. Actually in some unique way the younger ones may be even more gifted in this regard than their elders. They will repeat everything they have heard many, many times, either to each other or else to themselves. As a result everything gets recorded in people's memories; nothing is ever forgotten. To this store of information are added ideas and maxims which either crop up on the spur of the moment or else are dictated by the needs of urgent situations which people often have to face. Occasionally they will resort to this mental archive of theirs, but the stories which emerge always manage to sound exciting and important.

Al-Tiba relies for its livelihood on rain and agriculture and the thin strip of land which is irrigated by the spring. It's hardly surprising then that people always feel uneasy at the thought of the advent of years of drought. They make the most intensive preparations for such an eventuality by keeping a cow or two in every household or else a number of sheep. When the drought actually does come, they cannot even feed their own children, let alone animals. They proceed to unload a lot of their animal wealth on to shepherds and try to get rid of their remaining beasts by either slaughtering them or selling them off. There are actually fewer shepherds in al-Tiba than in a number of other villages, but they are skilful enough to be the envy of many people. A shepherd who is able to take the sheep of ten households out to pasture and knows what to do in the various seasons and where to take the animals will suddenly reappear during years of drought, even though he may have been out in the desert for a long time. He now has a particular hold over the owners of these sheep: he can sleep and reside in any house he likes without feeling the slightest bit shy or diffident. Shepherds like these have hidden talents which are not normally seen during good seasons. However, when drought comes, they become evident. The shepherds camp on the outskirts of the village. Some of them concentrate on hunting, but that does not make them lose the habits they have acquired as shepherds. People in al-Tiba have a truly remark-able knack for story-telling. They soon realize that these shepherds have lost the knack because they have been spending so much time with animals far out in the desert wastes. On the other hand, they are well aware that shepherds learn to deal with these prolonged periods of silence by singing wonderful songs. They accompany themselves on wooden instruments, and that is something which no one else can do really well. They even perform regularly at weddings and harvest festivals and on sad occasions too.

This is why shepherds become so indispensable during drought seasons and also because they know the places where animals are to be found. In general they are not very good at hunting, and no love is lost between them and real hunters. Shepherds are forever singing and playing those 'hellish' instruments (that is what the old people like to call them). They love showing off whenever possible, and never more so than when people are gathered together and some sort of performance is called for.

The village of al-Tiba marks the beginning of the desert proper. To the East are the orchards, the spring and then the market-place. The horizon marks the beginning of a chain of mountains. To the North and West broad plains stretch away into the distance interrupted once in a while by hills. These are sown with a wide variety of cereals and are also used to grow wheat, barley, vetch, clover and certain kinds of herbs. Close to the village itself vegetable greenery starts cropping up near the fruit trees. To the South the terrain becomes gradually more and more barren; the soil is flecked with outcrops of limestone chips. Bit by bit it changes. By the horizon it has turned into sand dunes, and then the desert itself starts. When the climate is good, al-Tiba is verdant and bursts into bloom on all sides. At the beginning of spring it is a riot of roses and other plants of all shapes and colours. Even the South side which seems so cruel and forbidding towards the end of summer manages to produce its own treasures from the bowels of the earth. People are at a loss to explain how all this can happen and how families in al-Tiba feel constrained at the beginning of spring to go out and pick all the incredible fruits which have till then remained buried beneath the ground. This entire festival season brings back memories of days of old when life was even more splendid and fruitful.

This particular village is marked by qualities and features which are not similarly bestowed on other villages around it. Even shepherds who have been given the responsibility of finding good pasturage will not venture close to al-Tiba's grazing grounds or traverse a fixed borderline. They know full well what the people in al-Tiba are like, the kind of temper which is their hallmark, and the stupid things they are liable to do if a stranger infringes on their means of sustenance or life-style.

People who live in al-Tiba know all about such things; in fact they constitute the villagers' trademark. Those who have to deal with them are also well aware of these traits. There are some villages which manage to produce many sons from their corporate belly, send them out all over the place and then lose track of them. With al-Tiba the whole thing is completely different. The village manages to engender in its children a kind of nostalgia which can never be forgotten. Even people who travel a lot and go far away never miss any opportunity to mention the village's name. They always hanker after the good old days and long to return to spend their final days there. Those who do not regard it in quite that light still think seriously about going back from time to time. They will spend a few days there having a wonderful time and reminiscing about things which happened in days of yore. They walk past every single house, sit in the market cafe and the other cafe by the spring, and take great gulps of the air, hoping that it will give them all the strength they need to face the future and persevere with that new life which they have begun elsewhere.

There were times when people liked to reminisce about the good old days. But the hard times also had a particular fascination of their own. Memory managed to turn even the greatest hardships into an odd type of heroism; so much so that people found it difficult to believe that they had actually managed to put up with everything and still carry on!

This sense of loyalty which people in al-Tiba feel towards their village home is not restricted to any one aspect nor indeed to the people who live there. People who leave the village to earn a living or to study elsewhere and who live in faraway places are not content simply to send home flour, sugar, letters and a few other items; they come back and spend a good deal of time there, especially when they fail to convince their relatives in the village to come and live with them in their new place of residence. The time they spend back in al-Tiba causes them a good deal of sorrow; that much is undeniably true. They cannot hide the sadness they feel, particularly when they notice that there is only a trickle of water from the spring and that the stream has run dry. They hear the sound of axes smashing into the trunks of dessicated trees, and the whole thing makes them feel as though they are the ones being throttled. Add to all this the tales of people who have moved away and been separated from friends and relatives, young and old, and the melancholy feelings of the returnees turn into a touch of nerves. The conversation takes a new tack: they start blaming and criticizing the old people, even though they themselves are much younger.

'We've told you hundreds of times,' they yell at the old people, 'this land's only good for feeding rats. That's all. But you people keep hanging on here as though it's paradise on earth. Give it all up and move to the city! You'll find life there a thousand times better than it is here!'

Silence ensues. The people living in al-Tiba, especially the older ones, will stare sadly at the people speaking to them. For a few moments it may appear as though they have never set eyes on those faces before and do not recognize to whom they belong. At other times the old people get the impression that they are listening to someone else or that the city has managed to corrupt them completely and made them talk that way.

The old people have an endless stream of pictures running through their minds: memories of al-Tiba in a wide variety of times, good and bad; when grass used to grow on the rocks and roofs of houses; when springs used to burst out of the ground all over the place. They would breathe in deeply as they recalled all these details. It was as if they could sense the smell of fertility being fostered in all living things, not merely human beings, but animals and minerals too. They remembered everything, but most of all they recalled how wonderful the food used to taste; and would that set the saliva flowing!

The village children had long since left al-Tiba and settled in the city far away. Even so they did not really mean everything they said. It was not deliberately rude. The thing which induced them to say these things and even more to act as they did was the way the same problems kept recurring. But, in spite of all the argument, the village offspring in their new homes kept mentioning al-Tiba. They would tell everyone what a fantastic village it was, unlike any other village in the entire region. Nor were they satisfied just to talk about the village. So strong was their sense of attachment that, on many occasions when nostalgia got the better of them, they would do the most unbelievable things. They would go back to the village to have their weddings and celebrate anniversaries. They used to send their sons there for the summer to spend some time living as they had done when they were young. And, when they themselves felt the urge, they would invite their friends to spend a few days in that wonderful region around al-Tiba.

'In al-Tiba the sky seems very close,' they would say, 'and it's as clear as can be. The nights bring their own thrill with them, something you can't match anywhere else in the whole world. When fresh fruit and dairy products are available, they're absolute heaven. Fresh skimmed butter, chicken, lamb cooked on a wood fire, all this and lots more besides; there's just nothing like the way they are in al-Tiba! And then there's the hunting! There's plenty of it to be had: partridge and rabbit, and even some wild species which have died out in most other places. All these and more you can find in the deep valleys around al-Tiba. There's lots of spring water to be had too. In years when the rainfall is plentiful, springs burst out through cracks in the ground and gush from under every rock. The water's cold and fresh; you can't drink enough of it!'

This is the way they would talk about the village. Whenever fruit from the village reached the city in small baskets, the village people who now lived there would keep turning it over again and again, just looking at it. They preferred offering it to guests and talking about it. Once in a while the conversation might turn to the subject of dairy products obtainable in the city, whereupon you would often see their expressions change. If you were quick off the mark, you might catch an expression which managed to combine disgust and nostalgia. For just a moment or two the impression would be left that the only food they could tolerate had to come from al-Tiba; nowhere else would do. A whole host of factors was at work in the hearts of both those who remained in the village and those who left. The resulting mixture is so complicated that it is quite impossible to explain.

Like many other places al-Tiba has sandy soil and often runs out of water. However there is something else which serves as a powerful tie. On long summer nights when the old people start talking, they use a kind of language which has a great appeal for those who have come out from the city.

'Many years ago,' they would start, 'the mountains around al-Tiba were as green as orchards. But then the Turks started building the railway and running trains through. They did not leave a single tree standing. They needed the timber and did not care where it came from. When the time came for them to leave, they burned down trees in the inaccessible spots on the tops of mountains simply because they could not get at them to cut them down. Those mountains, which, as you can see, are stripped bare all the way out from the city to al-Tiba, used to be green when we were youngsters. Horsemen could get lost in the thick forests which used to fill the plains close to al-Tiba.'

Tales like these would evoke any number of images in people's minds. The children of al-Tiba (who had already heard them a hundred times) used to love coaxing the old people into telling them over and over again, especially when they were entertaining guests from the city. In some obscure way they seemed eager to identify the precise quality which set their home village apart. Even though that quality may not have been quite as obvious at that particular moment as they would have liked, it lay hidden just beneath the surface somewhere and was bound to show itself.

'There's nothing better,' they would add craftily, 'than to spend your last days in this blessed village.'

The very same cunning would be used to induce the old people to talk about their ages. Some of the men used to enjoy this sort of chatter, but it alarmed the women. They would interrupt the conversation; sometimes they got quite worked up about it. But no sooner had the talk taken a serious turn again than the old people would be telling people how clear the air was and how fresh the water; what a good idea it was to go to bed and wake up early; what kinds of food they liked to eat; how dreadful the new types of disease were; the sudden and early death which seems to afflict life in the city; all things which they attributed to causes they had never encountered or heard of before.

Conversation in the evening would start quite spontaneously and without any pre-arrangement. It might be interspersed with a few innocent games. It would all happen on the spur of the moment with no prior planning. The process would include elaborate digressions. Things would always start with forests, trees, springs and so on. But then talk about periods of drought and the hardships the village had to face during those years would inevitably follow. Special feelings would be aroused by the sheer joy and pleasure which people felt during times of plenty when the ground was fertile, but the very mention of the hard times they lived through and survived would bring other sentiments rushing back, sentiments which overflowed with an assertive pride of a particular kind. Even children who had heard the stories over and over again would love to listen to them one more time; with every retelling they would sound fresh and packed full of heroic actions and lessons to be learned. 'We used to eat grass and plant roots,' the stories would go. 'We stooped to eating jerboas and even rats. Yes, they used to come into the village during drought years; in fact, they may have been the cause of such bad times. In those days that was the kind of thing we used to eat. Life was really tough, but men were men in those days: strong and hardy; they might even have eaten solid rocks! But the men today...!'

At this point some of the old people would smile. Others would reminisce. They would stare at each other and then glance at their children and lastly at their guests.

All this gives you some idea of what al-Tiba means to the people who are born there. When drought comes, everyone in the village feels a particular kind of sickness, and it makes no difference whether they are living there or far away. This sickness gradually becomes an obsession and then a nightmare. The villagers who now live far away need no prompting from anyone, if they can possibly afford it, to go back to the village.

But even such help as that is not enough to stave off the hardships and calamities which follow one another with alarming rapidity. The flow of water in the spring begins to slacken off, and the irrigation ditch slows down to a trickle and then dries up completely. The stream looks like a snake which has just died and is in the process of shedding its skin. Trees begin to droop and then dry up too. The apricot trees are the first to die, and others soon follow; walnut and olive crops are lost.

At such times al-Tiba looks brooding and ugly. Everything takes on a yellowish tinge. To the South there are no more truffles, mushrooms, sorrel, or a host of other types of fungi to be found. Indeed a whole series of sandstorms comes swirling in and covers everything in sight. The sky over the village is enveloped in a cloud of sickening dust. Swarms of flies and crows gather around the animal corpses and their droppings. People's voices turn into a muffled drone which bodes ill for everyone. In years such as this a number of people will certainly die, and many un-anticipated events occur.

Humans are not the only ones affected either. Animals and birds have a hard time too. Animals which cover a broad swathe of territory round the village will normally roam nonchalantly and lead a peaceful life. That makes them almost indifferent to the need for a full belly. But with the advent of drought they soon turn into totally different beasts: impetuous, restive and easily startled as they search for something to eat. Before long they turn into querulous and stubborn creatures, showing signs of temper and recalcitrance which can lead to actual harm. Eventually they become emaciated and sick. When that happens, their owners panic and try to get rid of them as soon as possible; they either slaughter them or else sell them off quickly. Birds used to traverse many a sky in search of sustenance. They had always continued on their way across the al-Tiba sky, almost as though, through some extraordinary process of heredity from ages past, some instinct deep down had taught them to pass over al-Tiba and go somewhere else. The only exception to this rule were the blasted desert birds which had such a vicious streak to them. They all seemed to abandon their normal category of haven in this world and head towards al-Tiba and its environs. From there they would wage their eternal battle against mankind for the remnants of crops and the few remaining drops of water.

Every town, city and village has its own types of madness and madmen. The al-Tiba brand came in numerous categories and each was something special. In drought seasons these categories would appear in more profusion than ever. The predominant category (to the point of being virtually the only one) concerned hunting. Those people who did not have this particular hobby regarded it with sentiments ranging from sheer contempt to outright disapproval. In their eyes it was virtually a declaration of stupidity and sloth. However when drought came, even these people would suddenly discover within themselves a hidden and painful yearning to become hunters of one kind or another. The motivations would vary: they might want to have a guaranteed supply of food; or else their interest might be in getting rid of the predatory birds and giving vent to their desire for revenge. After all, there might still be some seeds left in the ground which would grow the following year, or at least those same seeds might manage to produce a few green leaves which the hungry animals could eat. These may have been some of the motives, but then again the real reason might have been the desire to take vengeance on some enemy or other.

This particular year the maniacs in al-Tiba were more numerous and vociferous than ever. Even during the year of the great famine which had immediately followed the war, they had never appeared in such numbers and circumstances. The hunting season was barely under way before they were all getting their ancient rifles out of closets, dusting them off and cleaning them carefully. Then the planning and talking started. Nor was that all. They started devising new hunting techniques and used their ingenuity to manufacture bullets to their own design. Some of these lunatics had suffered from this particular disease from a long time back. Now they resorted to low cunning in order to wreak revenge on the old times when they had been the butt of al-Tiba's sarcasm. They dangled the temptations of hunting in front of everyone's eyes and convinced them all that this was the only way to save the community. Just to make sure their ploy would work, they distributed free ammunition which they themselves had manufactured in their own primitive way. Once they had people converted, they made use of them to prepare everything which would make their task easier.

'Nothing's simpler than hunting,' they would declare. 'To be a hunter, you have to practise; it's just like learning how to swim.'

At first, the people listening could not believe their ears. But gradually that hidden temptation worked its wiles and managed to suck many of them into the trap. Day by day more and more lunatics would join the group. These new conscripts would swell with pride whenever they shot down a bird. It only took a single day to turn them into zombies, people whose only idea of rest and relaxation was killing birds and chasing them hither and yon. That was how things got started. It was still fairly small-scaled and covert for the most part. Even so it managed to annoy many of the old people and those people who looked on hunting as a livelihood and a means of just staying alive.

In circumstances like these a better way of describing the sport is utter irresponsibility. It was certainly not something which men who appreciated their duties should have been doing. They should have been more concerned about the major problems which were becoming more acute every day. But the phenomenon kept growing. Those who at first seemed a little hesitant soon gave way, particularly when they saw dozens of grouse being brought in. When they turned the birds over to see how much flesh they had on them, they would voice their disappointment. 'Pretty poor,' they would say. 'Much worse than in previous years, that's for sure.' To prove a point, they would turn the birds over again and start squeezing the breasts. But these extra gestures and the pressure of their fingers on that fresh meat would bring about a change in their attitude too. They would start feeling tempted. With each new catch their diffidence would recede a little further. No words or pronouncements were to be heard, but each one of them made his own private decision to start hunting.

It was the same story with the old people. At first they kept yelling angrily at the hunters; the whole stupid thing they regarded as a kind of infatuation, certainly not something men should be involved in during a gruesome period of trial such as this. But even they relented before long. True enough, they did not do it either openly or quickly. But their opposition began to crumble and, as days went by, it dwindled away to nothing. Their comments now assumed a muted tone, something akin to advice:

'Why don't you go to the city and find work there? What's the point of gallivanting all over this dust-ridden area and wandering around the mountains and desert just to look for a few starving birds when they are all sinew and feathers in any case? It's all a big waste of time!'

The younger people would nod their heads to acknowledge that they had been listening, but the gesture implied neither agreement nor disagreement. In such contexts some of the old people would add a short postscript: 'When calamity strikes, it only comes once.'

And so the sport kept expanding in scope. The young men organized everything they needed for the next day's hunting. They would get ammunition ready, clean the guns and put pieces of coloured cloth filled with holes on sticks as lures for the birds. When the old people noticed what was going on and realized that the young people were not to be dissuaded, they changed their tone. Now their voices sounded more affectionate and scared as well:

'You should be more careful, you know. That bird-shot chews everything up, dead or alive.'

They watched the way the bullets were being put together to be sure the young men were not making mistakes. Once they had been reassured, they would repeat one particular phrase over and over again: 'That great maniac, 'Assaf. He's the one who's to blame for all this misery.'

Men and women, young and old, everyone in the village knew 'Assaf. Even so he was something of a mystery. People rarely set eyes on him or had a chance to sit down and chat with him. He was between forty and fifty years old, tall, but with a slight stoop. He looked skinny but had a powerful physique. He was a bachelor, and people argued a lot about the reasons why. Some people maintained that he had wanted to marry his cousin, but her father had refused point blank because 'Assaf had had no job and could not support himself, let alone a wife and family. The story that other people told was that the girl herself had refused and had even threatened to set herself on fire if they compelled her to marry him. The reasons she gave were that he was eccentric and cruel. When her mother was questioned about it later on, she too made it clear that she had been totally opposed to the whole idea. Her daughter's shoes, to quote her own words, were worth as much as the head of that layabout who spent his entire life wandering around in the desert and in caves. She went on to say that he was crazy too. Anyone who took the trouble to investigate the matter further would have discovered other reasons as well. The entire issue kept al-Tiba occupied for a while, but it all came to a peaceful and quiet end. No one even talks about it any more. The one result of the episode was a name for 'Assaf, Abu Layla. With the passage of time any people who still express any interest in the matter have changed their attitude to a flippant sarcasm, all the more so since 'Assaf adamantly refuses to answer any questions on the subject.

This then is the way people have come to regard 'Assaf. At this juncture they would find it odd to see him presented any other way.

Hunting had been one of his main interests ever since he was a boy. Year by year as he grew older, the interest developed along with him. When he was young, the whole thing was on a simple and primitive level; he used to do exactly the same things that boys of his age will always do. However of all the boys of his age he was the one with the greatest interest in hunting. When his father died, he became totally involved in this risky pastime. The things which boys normally do no longer amused him. He would imitate the older men and go wherever they went. He was forever trying to devise new hunting techniques; as a result he acquired some habits which made him seem somewhat eccentric. He would spend much of his time in orchards. He started smoking at a very early age. He spent long periods contemplating the realms of nature, human beings and the animals all around him. Most of the time he would avoid people. When he was in their midst, the weapon he would use against them was silence.

As he grew up, these traits grew with him. When his mother died, his temperament altered even more drastically than before. Instead of coming back into the village and behaving like everyone else, sowing, reaping and leading a sedentary life, he purchased an old kind of hunting rifle. It seemed very peculiar for a boy of just thirteen to be copying older people, spending all his time on his own outside the village and moving from one mountain or valley to another.

Beyond these details about 'Assaf's childhood, almost nothing is known about large segments of his life. If he himself had ever felt in the mood for reminiscing, he would not have been able to remember anything about more than a tiny fraction of it. Even then, the only major events would all be connected with hunting: where he had shot the wolf and how he had managed to do it; when snowfall had piled up in drifts and blocked all roads and made travel difficult; how many times he had had to sleep in caves for fear of dying of exposure. He could also remember the number of times he had refused to shoot at a female partridge because she was herding a gaggle of young ones in front of her. No one else was particularly interested in these memories and others like them. Even if he felt like telling some more stories, they would always sound weird and convoluted; he could not maintain the necessary momentum.

People like him change gradually day by day; they become even more eccentric and introspective. It was his very nature that led him to prefer staying out of other people's way. It was almost as though he lived in his own private world with its own particular problems and did not feel like sharing them with anyone else. He had a harsh and offhand way of expressing himself; if you did not understand the way he was or know how to respond, it could sometimes sound offensive.

Al-Tiba knew many different kinds of people, and so it got used to 'Assaf just as it did with everyone else. No one felt alarmed or threatened by his scruffy clothes and taciturn demeanour, or even by the string of oaths he would unleash from time to time when someone pinned him down and started firing provocative questions at him. People initially regarded him with a leering kind of sarcasm, and that turned eventually into laughter.

'Assaf himself got used to living like this and found it very hard to change his ways. On those few occasions when he had to get some different clothes, he would behave in the most incredible fashion, doing things which no one in their right mind would even contemplate. For example, when his shoes wore out and he had to buy a new pair, he would not put them on immediately; several adjustments had to be made so as to alter them in certain respects. Where the two smallest toes were, he used to cut the leather, put the shoes in water, and then beat them hard on the ground. If anyone had the nerve to ask 'Assaf why he was doing this, he had no reply. Even he had no idea why he was doing it. If it were just shoes that were involved, there would have been no particular problem; somehow everyone would have understood. But he did something like this to all his clothing. He used to rip his trousers in several places and then sew a number of colourful patches over the holes; sometimes he even used a piece of soft leather.

This was the way he was, and no one could persuade him to do otherwise. During the major festivals he had to make the round of all the homes in al-Tiba, as people have been doing since time immemorial. But, unlike everyone else, he would do nothing to change his appearance. In fact, he would actually go to enormous lengths to wear the scruffiest clothes he could find in his tiny room. That incidentally was the only place he had left once he had sold off first the orchard and then parts of the house itself. The interior room and a small vegetable garden were all that was left.

People in al-Tiba got used to 'Assaf. With the passage of time and a growing familiarity with his ways, he no longer prompted questions or signs of disapproval. The only thing which did attract their attention (but even that did not last for long) was when he acquired a dog. When people asked him about it, he used to go on at great length about the animal's importance and pedigree; he would grossly inflate the amount of money he had paid for it. On several occasions people claimed that 'Assaf had found the creature as a stray and that it may have wandered away from some other hunter. In any case 'Assaf had brought the dog back with him. Other people in al-Tiba went so far as to suggest that 'Assaf had actually stolen the dog. 'Assaf himself would listen to some of the things people kept saying about him, but his only response would be to give an insouciant smile and pat the dog's back affectionately.

'Just listen to those imbeciles!' he would tell the dog. 'Do you hear what they're saying?'

At that time 'Assaf spent longer than usual inside his house and then stayed in al-Tiba for two whole weeks without going out to hunt. People had explanations for this: he was scared, they claimed. Those with the theory that the dog was stolen were merely confirmed in their suspicions. If there were any other reason, they suggested, 'Assaf would not be so afraid to go out hunting and to take the dog with him. Other people were of the opinion that 'Assaf had just found the dog somewhere. They felt sure the animal would go back to its owners as soon as it managed to get out of the house and regain its freedom of movement. There would be absolutely nothing 'Assaf could do if the dog ran away and went back to its rightful owners. The truth of the matter is that 'Assaf only felt sure when he did things for himself. Now it so happened that some hunters came in to al-Tiba from far away. He took them out, expended a great deal of energy on them, showed them the right places to hunt partridge, and let them keep five birds which he had shot himself. The hunters gave him the dog as a present, but 'Assaf did not have complete confidence in the animal. He spent a great deal of time training it, and that made people in al-Tiba laugh at him. In fact at that period they were laughing at just about everything he did and especially the amount of time he spent inside the house. He used to tie a rope on the dog and then start taking it on walks around the neighbourhood. He bought the dog some 'bitter-sweet' and tried to teach it new habits. Everyone who saw him dragging the dog around on the end of a rope had a hearty laugh.

'Just look at the idiot,' they all commented with malicious

glee, 'he's keeping a hunting dog on a leash!'

'How are we supposed to tell who's doing the hunting or helping whom!'

That was not all either. Now they all joined the other people in believing that 'Assaf had stolen the dog. If that were not the case, they argued, he would not be going to all this trouble.

'Heaven help us! Perhaps they're actually siblings! After all, they do look exactly alike, don't they?'

All this belongs to the recorded history of al-Tiba, something which has almost faded from people's memories by now. Once 'Assaf and the dog became attached to one another, the image of the two of them became as one. Some spiteful characters even went so far as to suggest that there was a close resemblance between 'Assaf and the dog: they both had a large nose and big ears, and the sound of their voices was muted, rather like a gurgling noise. Needless to say, no one could say anything of the kind to 'Assaf directly or even when he was around. Even so, everyone called the dog 'Assaf too and stared at it in a particular way.

Al-Tiba is no different from any number of other towns and villages in the unkindness and sarcastic wit which its inhabitants can exhibit and in its desire to make up jokes and fabricate lies about others. People love talking about the way other people spend time away, especially if they are like 'Assaf. When someone spots him at almost the first light of dawn, a somewhat sarcastic grin will cross his face as he asks 'Assaf a series of questions about hunting, the dog, and the incredible things he sees in the desert.

Talk will continue far into the night, and there will always be lots of stories. Someone is bound to volunteer a piece of information along these lines:

'I saw 'Assaf today with the dog on his back!'

'I spotted the real 'Assaf today,' someone else will chip in, cackling with laughter as he does so. 'There he was hunting, rifle in hand. That's the real 'Assaf, not the other phoney one!'

''Assaf took a shot at a male partridge once,' a third person put in, 'but he missed and hit the dog instead. That's why it's only got one eye!'

In fact, something had happened at one point. But the

story-telling techniques in al-Tiba are different from elsewhere in the region. If every story told by someone from al-Tiba is supposed to contain a certain amount of truth, then it has to be admitted that the dog's eye was missing from the very first day it arrived in al-Tiba. That was the way 'Assaf accepted the dog; he did not ask how or when it had happened. One day he said it might have happened while hunting, but he did not go into details. People in al-Tiba took up the tale and went on to say that it had happened to 'Assaf himself and with this very same dog. If there had been an occasion when 'Assaf was forced to carry his dog, it was because the animal had been involved in a vicious fight with a wolf, one in which 'Assaf had almost been killed as well. The dog had been mangled in several places. If it had been left behind, it would certainly have died. As for the tale which some people in al-Tiba tell about seeing 'the real 'Assaf', namely the dog, carrying the rifle and hunting with it – well, there's no foundation to it whatsoever! It is simply a piece of fantasy tinged with sheer envy. The dog was so highly trained that it could help by carrying some of the game his master had taken (such as a male partridge) in its teeth.

Al-Tiba will enjoy a good joke just as much as any other village when times are good and people feel relaxed. But things soon change when times are fraught with worries. When the rain stops and drought moves in, this change is a drastic one. The village seems to have gone into mourning. At sunset it looks shrouded in darkness. A wave of mournful silence pervades the entire area. Nights seem long and quiet, broken only by the forlorn howling of hungry stray dogs and the occasional shot. At such times the air over al-Tiba becomes polluted by a heavy and alarming smell which is only recognized by people who know it well and have smelled it before. At such times many things change.

There has never been a year like this one before; that much was obvious from the very first days of winter. Normally all the villages which lie on the edge of the desert expect early rains. These rains herald a fruitful season and bring with them an untold number of desert plants (which, some people claim, fall down from heaven along with the rain itself!). This year however there were no rains, but instead bitterly cold winds. People in al-Tiba were used to dealing with cold winters and were not unduly bothered or disturbed by the whole thing. After all, it was still the beginning of winter, and there would surely be many good long days ahead. But the older people knew better. They had experienced the caprices of nature before and knew how to distinguish harbingers of a good season from warning signs of drought. They started to get worried, a sensation which was actually more akin to sorrow. Bad times from previous years came flooding back into their minds, bringing with them memories of calamities and illnesses, followed by death. Even so they managed to suppress all such premonitions and memories and said nothing. The younger men who had had less experience of nature and its seasons looked quizzically up at the sky, wondering whether the things they knew could be of any use at all in this type of situation. Children started asking their parents if there would be mushrooms, truffles, sorrel, mallow and dozens of other types of desert plant around this year, but the men simply stared back at them in dismay. It was almost like having to answer difficult exam questions. The answers they gave their children were vague and almost provocative.

'It's only just the beginning of winter,' they said, 'and here you all are with a disease we didn't even know about when we were your age: you've all got unanswerable-questions disease!'

Needless to say, the youngsters were not satisfied with such stonewalling. They went to ask their mothers and plied them with endless questions.

'When are we going out to the desert, mother?'

'When are we going to pick mushrooms?'

'Will there be as many truffles this year as in previous years?'

Children at that particular age probably did not dare to keep nagging their fathers with questions and arguing with them, but it was much worse for their mothers. The women did their best; in their own mysterious way they used every means at their disposal to parry this line of questioning, a process which involved not a little sheer cunning. But promises had already been made, and little minds were working at fever pitch on dozens of dreams and desires. When the mothers glanced at the men and particularly the older people, they could read in their expressions signs of hard times to come and miseries which would not be easily forgotten.

This then is the way winter began this year. One day would follow another, and yet no rain would fall. People going out to the field would feel more and more uneasy and glance mournfully at the soil. The cold had made the ground rock hard. Twittering birds arrived in large numbers and set up a non-stop barrage of sound from dawn till dusk; they would peck around, oblivious to the scarecrows which had been put up at several points in the fields. Every day would bring with it some new warning sign. People began to get even more anxious. Women in particular started to feel downhearted. When the weather turned stormy and the cold winds blew, the village would be gripped by an agonizing feeling of impending doom, just like a razor's edge.

'Will these winds bring any rain?'

'Will anything grow after all this dry weather? Even if we get a drop or two of rain now, is there any guarantee we'll get some more in March and April?'

People had other kinds of questions on their minds too. 'Once this season's over, God should send us some early spring rain. If that happens, we'll get something to eat from the desert and save ourselves the risk of exhaustion and even death. But it's already too late for that. March is almost over and gone without a single drop of rain. Who can tell how life'll turn out now that this has happened?'

But at the very end of March it did rain. It was plentiful and lasted for two whole days. For that short time people's expressions changed and so did their behaviour. Even those who had nothing in particular to do with agriculture looked happier and sometimes gave vent to their feelings in quite lighthearted ways. Many people made so bold as to suggest that this year's season, and particularly the summer part, would be the best ever. However those people who worked the land and knew nature's caprices said nothing and were not very optimistic. They were waiting for something else. No sooner had the sun risen on the third day than they stopped any more early seasonal planting and proceeded to plough as quickly as possible. In doing so, they, like everyone else, made use of every means at their disposal to guarantee themselves a good crop!

The old people were neither convinced nor delighted by this plentiful, almost frenzied rainfall at the end of March. They were of an entirely different ilk, one fashioned perhaps by nature itself and by those long days and the apprehensions which went along with them. Or perhaps there were other yet more obscure reasons connected with the very soil itself. Each one of them realized that every passing day brought him closer and closer to the earth. As long as that was the case, each and every one of them felt impelled by a secret desire for a piece of earth which could receive his flesh and bones when he died. The very same feeling made him realize deep down inside that the aridity which was gradually infiltrating the soil and the slimy mud which the March rains had caused were both unsuitable for his eventual plans. As a result, each one of the old people was anxious not to die in a harsh year like this one. The mean tricks which nature could play made them feel desperate, anxious and even weary of the whole thing, but nevertheless each one of them wanted to die a decent and noble death, to pass away quietly and peacefully after fulfilling all the obligations of this life; and all this to be achieved without any fuss, but with all the respect due someone of his age. The very idea of dying the way young people or even animals did, suddenly and without any kind of warning, would drive them to the most profound feelings of despair.

Things turned out exactly as the old people had predicted. The abundant rains which fell at the end of March moistened the seeds deep down in the soil. They all started to grow and soon broke through the surface soil. Many seeds had been lost to the birds, and the ploughs had made deep furrows; as a result the plants sprouted at some distance from each other. Even so, they looked strong and sturdy. When the April sun bathed them in its warmth, they really came to life and grew even more. The farmers, filled with illusory optimism, kept repeating that what they really needed was a couple of rainfalls in April, one in the first half and another towards the end of the month, and then one final one in mid-May. All this optimism was an attempt on their part to convince themselves, no one else. In any case all such hopes were to be forlorn. From the very outset this year kept providing ample warnings of drought to come. The old people kept telling themselves the same thing. 'Assaf kept saying it out loud to everyone. If anyone bothered to ask him what was making him say such things, his answer would be neither clear nor convincing. 'Just you wait!' he would remark. 'That's all I have to say. You'll see for yourselves soon enough!'

When people heard 'Assaf talking that way, they began to get nervous and short-tempered, almost to the point of picking a quarrel. But deep down inside they realized that this maniac 'Assaf was saying things quite unlike what other people were saying. There was some truth to it, a hidden truth probably connected with things about which they knew absolutely nothing.

And then, mirroring what old people had sensed and anticipated, people started mouthing cautionary phrases; the words just seemed to slip out. They were followed by expressions of genuine alarm, accompanied by crystal-clear statements, things like:

'This year will be one of the worst al-Tiba has ever lived through.'

'I can't recall we've ever had a year like this one in al-Tiba,' one of them commented after a pause for thought and some gruesome reminiscing.

And that is precisely the way things turned out, exactly as the old people and 'Assaf·had told them it would!

People in al-Tiba felt an all-pervasive anxiety, and the sensation grew worse day by day. But 'Assaf did not allow himself to stay still or relax. He would arrive back in the village at sunset with dozens of birds, but never gave himself a moment's rest before starting to knock on people's doors. He would choose the houses carefully. Actually he would have given the matter a lot of thought well in advance. Even before the shot was fired at a bird, his intention would be clear: 'You're for Umm Sabri,' 'You're for Da'ud the blind man,' 'You're for Sa'id who's no good at anything except having daughters!'

These are the kinds of things 'Assaf would say to himself while hunting. When he went round the village knocking on people's doors, he was anxious not to scare people by making them think the very worst: maybe that a friend or relative had died, or something like that. So, before the door was opened, he used to yell out: 'It's 'Assaf. I've come to spend the evening with you!' And without waiting to listen to the torrent of abuse which would descend on him, he would leave a few birds and be on his way!

He used to do this every single night. He would leave just one bird for himself; on occasion there would be none left at all. When he had finished his task, he would start preparing ammunition for the next day's hunting, working by the light of a small lantern. This was a task where neither exhaustion nor interruption could be excused or condoned. It was late in the evening by the time he had finished. After a quick bite to eat he would soon be sound asleep and snoring his head off. He used to have any number of dreams, each one filled with myriad pictures. What was al-Tiba like then and now, he would ask himself. Why does life get more difficult day by day? Images of trees and birds would waft by, followed by a non-stop flow of water and spring blanketing endless spaces with its blooms and colours. Then he would see everything in flight; the entire sky would be full of birds. Hunters would only hunt in season, and then only those birds which needed to be hunted. Then there would be images of people who had died. When rain started falling, he began to worry that the ground would get waterlogged and he would not be able to get back. He started running ... That made him start in his sleep, and he woke up, feeling scared that time might indeed have passed him by. He could feel the dusty atmosphere in the room and rubbed his eyes so that he could check on the time. He had an internal clock of his own which never went wrong. All these years, summer and winter, it had never let him down. People used to come out from the city. They would make copious preparations to go hunting with 'Assaf: they would set alarm clocks and give the strictest instructions that they were to be woken up at the right time. They were worried that 'Assaf might leave them behind and go on his way. His pretext would always be that the sun was up and the day was being wasted; he used to tell them that they needed to be in the target area by sunrise. These people would always get the time wrong, whereas 'Assaf never did; his clock was always automatically right!

For ages and ages 'Assaf had been used to hunting on his own, taking only his dog with him. But even he found it hard to refuse to take other people with him, especially if they were guests or during years of drought. He would have much preferred to be on his own. But what was he supposed to do when the ground had completely dried up, the clouds had long since vanished, and people had nothing left to eat? Previously he had kept certain hunting grounds to himself and vowed he would never show them to anybody or even let anyone else get close to them. But now even he could not keep them a secret long. Even so, he used to issue stern warnings:

'Don't shoot at the females. They're the ones which give us all the rest!'

He was not always convinced they fully understood. 'The females,' he would add, 'I mean the female partridges, are smaller, and their colouring is more subtle.'

Even then they might still ask for more clarification and information. 'Like some human beings,' he would continue, 'the partridge cock is a coward.' He would stare at them all and laugh. 'It gets very scared. It has very bright colours, much brighter than the hen. And it will fly off before she does!'

They would all nod their heads in acknowledgement, but 'Assaf still had his doubts about these hunters. He particularly disliked the cowards and tricksters among them. But what worried him more than anything was that one day al-Tiba might find nothing to hunt at all.

'These birds belong to us,' he would say with some anxiety. 'Either for today or tomorrow. If we're careful about conserving them, they'll be here for us to hunt. But if we kill them all or hunt them too much, they'll make an end of it and look for somewhere else to live.'

He pictured a land totally devoid of partridges to hunt.

'Listen, you people,' he yelled testily. 'If these birds disappear and we get a year of drought, and if the government keeps telling us a pack of lies year after year and not building that dam, you can be sure that the people of al-Tiba are going to die, the whole lot of them. I'm convinced of that. How can any decent person kill human beings or birds just for fun?'

This kind of conversation would be heard at the start of every hunting trip. But in spite of everything, 'Assaf felt himself compelled to take a veritable caravan of hunters to the spots where partridges were to be found. Most of the time he would resort to a certain amount of cunning. He used to take them to the more out-of-the-way, risky and difficult areas, knowing full well that, when hunters feel tired or scared, they lose a lot of their more rapacious instincts and become more considerate. That, at any rate, was the way he had things planned at the start of the season. However life in al-Tiba soon became even rougher than usual; hunger began to impinge and take its toll of some people. 'Assaf paused long and hard before breaking many of the bounds which he had imposed on both himself and others. But eventually he had no choice. It used to break his heart. He unleashed a whole stream of curses and proceeded to do a whole series of stupid things.

'Look!' he used to say to justify the terrible wrong he was committing, 'if people don't eat the partridges, the jackals and wolves will get them anyway. Even if some of the damned animals managed to get away, shepherds would still come and pick up the eggs. People in al-Tiba mustn't be allowed to die!'

He had his own particular philosophy which had been formed and honed by both time and experience. Even if he had been willing to explain what was going on inside his mind, he would not have been able to do so. If he were asked why he was doing this or that, he would look baffled. 'That's what hunting is all about,' he would say. 'That's the way real hunters do things.' And that would be it!

This then was the way he would deal with the question of hunting. He followed this philosophy himself and expected everyone else to do the same. When the season for migratory birds arrived, he would feel profoundly relieved and gratified.

'All of you buckle down now!' he used to say, enunciating

clearly so that everyone could hear him. 'Every hunter has to prove himself!'

His aim in making this statement was to take the minds of other hunters off partridges. Actually they were already tired of hunting the bird. Their feet had become sore from clambering up high rock cliffs and penetrating far into remote valleys. Deep down they positively welcomed his suggestion and wholeheartedly supported it.

''Assaf's the best hunter around,' they would tell themselves and others by way of justifying their actions. 'If that's what he has to say, then we should certainly believe him and go along with his suggestion.'

'Assaf was anxious that the whole thing should not be seen as a trick, pure and simple. He used to take them out to the place where migratory birds would be found and to other spots where they would fly over. He never stinted about providing them all with the information they might need to help them get a larger bag of birds. Through some obscure process of admiration they flocked round him and let him take them wherever he decided and at whatever hour of the day. That way he made sure some partridges were left alive in remote areas.

'Once they feel secure again and realize that the gunshots have stopped,' he told himself confidently, 'they'll return to their nesting-grounds and live in peace again. The eggs will hatch, and a new batch of chicks will populate the mountains and valleys again!'

Actually 'Assaf is well aware of the fact that every animal and bird can defend itself; it knows where to go when danger threatens. It is just that, as he watched novice hunters getting more and more rapacious and thoughtless, breaking every rule in the book as they did so, he used to reflect sorrowfully that in the end people would die because partridges might well disappear.

'They kept hunting gazelles until they'd killed them all off,' he added after a long silence. 'The desert's been turned into one gigantic graveyard; the only things it produces are dust and death. People in al-Tiba have got to learn to be more intelligent than other people and not just kill everything off.'

In years like this one some unknown instinct would teach

partridges how to disappear; not even 'Assaf could explain it. They could make it look as though they had become extinct for good, as though they would never reappear in the future, clucking like chickens as they meandered around the feet of the mountains to the East. When this happened, you would notice a distinct transformation in the hunters, even the most stubborn of the novices. This abrupt change would be helped along by the fact that day by day desert birds, and particularly grouse, would start moving closer to al-Tiba. These timid birds would be made more reckless by their fruitless search for seeds and water; and that made them easy targets. Even small boys in the village could take pot shots at them with whatever primitive weapons they had managed to manufacture for their own use. At certain times of day the boys could even sneak up and bag a number of birds!

However the power of life itself was stronger still. Even the grouse, which is a really stupid bird, gradually learned some tricks of its own. It may well have been both hungry and thirsty, but by now another force had taken over and was calling the shots. Reckless grouse, which at the beginning of the season could be killed in tens and hundreds and could not tell a hunter from a peasant, rapidly became more cautious. At the outset hunters would treat them with total contempt and use any number of rude expressions to describe them: how tough the flesh was; how stupid it was; how hunting it was no fun. As days went by, these people would find themselves gradually drawn into a chase for it, at which point they had to come up with some excuse for their behaviour.

'It got hit and ran away,' they would intone loudly with that arrogance which is the hallmark of all hunters when they have been fooled. 'Now it's even more cautious than other birds!'

'It's more difficult than hunting partridges,' others would add assertively.

This is the way things start to change. Al-Tiba is living through some pretty hard times these days and looking for some way to remain alive. That is why it chooses to turn a blind eye to any number of things, such as the reckless behaviour of its young people and the way they gallivant off to hunt with an abandon which is as unprecedented as it is unanticipated.

Every so often the young people organize evening gatherings, and that surprises no one. At these meetings they agree on the places where they have to go and the methods they will use to hunt a large number of birds, especially grouse and partridges. They spend a lot of time talking about the mistakes of the past which need to be avoided. 'Assaf rarely participates in these sessions. He cannot be bothered with them; after all he knows where to go and when. When the young people start questioning him about places to go and techniques to use, the replies which he gives them are both terse and dogmatic:

'This madness clogging your brains will be the death of all the game that's left.'

He pauses for a moment. 'The hard times haven't even arrived yet,' he continues in that brash and severe tone which is his hallmark. 'We should be getting ready for them!'

This suggestion is greeted with scoffs of protest and accusations of running away when things get difficult.

'If you've an ounce of self-control left,' he will respond emotionally, 'I suggest you save your bullets. The grouse will come to you; you don't have to go looking for them!'

But the youngsters will not listen. Powerful hidden forces seem to be impelling them to take revenge; they feel the need for some kind of challenge.

Al-Tiba pays the price for such urges. At the beginning of the season the birds would not be worried about their own safety and would come in close. But they soon became scared and started looking for other feeding-grounds or else changing the times of day when they would arrive and depart. In a word, the birds learned to adjust their life-style. Life became more taxing and difficult for every living creature. 'Assaf himself used to come back to the village with large numbers of birds, but even he had to face the same forces as the novice hunters. His bag started to dwindle. Hunting turned into an exhausting activity, more like an expedition.

Even so, 'Assaf is not one to take a rest!

And so began the harsh, grim days. Al-Tiba had long since

made up its mind to be located in that particular part of the world, right on the edge of the desert. The self-same process made it select hunting and a life full of courage. The village learned year by year how to endure all kinds of difficulties and calamities.

In most places droughts would lead to rifts between people; everyone would be looking for some way to guarantee a slice of bread for himself. In al-Tiba on the other hand droughts and other miseries only brought people closer together; the whole community became a single family, one body united. True enough, there was a small group of people who came from somewhere far away, chose to settle in al-Tiba, and carried on working and behaving with all the disinterest and suspicion of total strangers (in spite of everything which al-Tiba was offering them). But, if you discounted them, everyone faced the hardships with a spirit of cooperation and sharing; and that made things seem less grim and easier to cope with. This remarkable process, involving as it did a kind of tacit heroism, meant that no one was allowed to die without the utmost effort being made to help him. In most cases this was done so surreptitiously that no one even noticed. At some time of day or night households with families so large that they could not face up to the realities of life would leave their doors open. Amounts of wheat or little portions of sugar, tea and soap would be tossed inside. People who had given up everything they owned to buy seeds or other things from the city found themselves offered help which was not available to those who were more self-sufficient. The disabled and handicapped were taken care of by a number of young people who would cook their food for them; more often than not it would be a soup broth or shepherd's pie. Widowed women would get a tremendous amount of attention at such times. Al-Tiba could normally feed its children pieces of meat, but with such limited resources it could not afford to be so generous in the face of such difficult times year after year. The old people kept warning everyone not to be extravagant. They urged everyone to conserve as much as possible and to regard the times al-Tiba was living through as a period of plenty, one which would be followed by a rapidly accumulating mound of hardships. But the village carried on as usual, basing its activities on some obscure hope; it was as though they were all waiting for something or other to happen. Needless to say, this hope never came to fruition, as many imagined it would. Instead the wait turned into one prolonged torment!

The young people from the village who were living far away in the big city did not wait for the cries for help to arrive. They rushed to offer whatever assistance they could. They sent back wheat, barley, lentils, sugar, tea and soap. They also sent messages to members of their family and friends, suggesting that they come to the city and stay with them for a while. But such proposals were entirely unacceptable to people in al-Tiba, particularly the old people. They could not conceive of the idea of going away and leaving others to die of starvation or thirst. The very idea provoked a feeling of shame which was utterly intolerable. They did not respond to the letters from the city or accept the invitations which were offered. The children who had left the village but stayed in touch knew full well that what they were suggesting was well nigh impossible and that no one would accept the invitation. As a result they went to enormous lengths to offer all the help they could. Soon afterwards they started flocking back to the village themselves. At first they came just for a visit, but the purpose would soon turn into a strong desire to participate somehow in the process of facing this bitter disaster. After all they might be able to do something or at least learn. The visits would be extended for several days and repeated at increasingly close intervals. The motivation involved was not merely sentimental attachment or even a kind of masochism. Many other things arrived along with these returnees: extra portions of wheat and barley, linen clothes, and along with all that, promises and a generous helping of sheer verbiage. It was always these promises that everyone in al-Tiba found the hardest to tolerate. This year in particular they turned into an unbearable form of torture.

'Before you know it,' the word would be, 'they'll be building the dam. Once it's finished, al-Tiba will never be hungry or thirsty again.'

That is precisely the sort of thing that influential types in the capital used to say. 'Before autumn's over,' they would go on, 'and the rainy season starts, machinery will start digging up the ground and lining the rocks up in piles. Hundreds of workmen and engineers will arrive. You'll see the whole thing with your very own eyes!'

People in al-Tiba were quite prepared to accept whatever was sent out to them and to distribute it with scrupulous fairness. They used to listen to this talk from the big city. They would hear all about the earth dam which was due to be built close to al-Tiba: it would be able to retain all the water which poured down during certain seasons and finished up in the bowels of the earth. No one could imagine how all that water could simply vanish or where it went. All that was left of these torrents were pebbles and deep trenches where large clumps of soil and vegetable-patches had been washed away. Big words and empty promises, they were the other things left behind!

In al-Tiba people listened to all this talk in a rueful silence. They could not make up their minds whether their children and the other men who locked themselves up inside big buildings were lying to them.

'We've heard this stuff so many times before,' they would tell themselves. 'Years have gone by, and nothing has changed.'

When times were good, they forgot all about the dam, the road and electricity. It would never occur to them that they might be given such modern conveniences. But when drought came, they would remember every detail: what the men who had come looked like and what it was they said. Something else jogged their memories too. Friends of their children had come to al-Tiba as visitors in previous years when the soil had been fertile and produce was good. They had gone hunting in areas around the village and had come back so overjoyed that at some points they had behaved more like children. They had seemed sincere enough. Some of these people were now important senior officials in the distant city, so much so that their names were mentioned in the same breath as those of prophets and saints. However they no longer had any memory of al-Tiba;

they had forgotten all about their friends who lived there. It was all over.

In drought seasons al-Tiba was left to lick its own wounds. But, when times were good, the village would send baskets of apricots into the city at the beginning of the season and towards the end would follow them up with grapes and dates. In between there would be yoghourt, cheese, eggs and young lamb as well. Nothing was expected from the city in return. Al-Tiba would send these things in to the city with a feeling of pleasure bordering on sheer joy. Fathers and mothers would send in baskets and bags of yoghourt on the small bus which used to leave for the city in the early morning. For them it was a solemn obligation. If they missed the departure of the employees' bus by just a minute or so, or else were unable to pick the dates at the appropriate moment, they were bitterly sorry!

So there was al-Tiba, unchanged and constant, forever loyal to everything in it and to every single person who lived there or passed by. The village managed to forge in its children an exceptional sense of loyalty, something which was unparalleled in any other villages whether close by or further away. During this cursed and dire year a large number of al-Tiba's sons came back to the village. No pleas or hints were required. As their feet touched the soil in al-Tiba and their eyes fell on the houses, they were filled with a profound sense of sorrow and chided themselves inwardly for waiting so long. The comparison between their life in the city and that of the people in al-Tiba gave them a guilty conscience. However, these initial feelings of sadness and regret soon gave way to a powerful desire to do something. Perhaps this time al-Tiba would be saved; then it might survive until the dam was built. Maybe something would happen in the big city which would make it possible for them to face the cruelties of nature without having to wait for false promises of the fickle rainfall which came year after year and then failed them for years.

As soon as people arrived from the city, they would take off their city clothes and put on the things they had worn years ago in the village. During the daytime they would pass by most of the houses in the village and enquire after the people who lived there. They would grieve for those who had died, ponder over the whole host of suggestions which would be made to them, and make several private resolutions as to what they would do when they got back to the city. But that was not all. They distributed the things they had brought with them and started writing whole series of letters to relatives and friends in the distant city and even in the United States. At night they would spend a lot of time thinking and talking, but with every word they uttered there came a profound feeling of bitterness because they could not be sure about anything!

When needed al-Tiba could display tremendous patience and tolerance. Strangers could be forgiven just as much as its own citizens. But in drought seasons anger could be seen as well, the kind of anger which sometimes might seem like a trifling matter but which would eventually turn into an inconceivable and indeed intolerable kind of madness.

For example, a young man who was studying far away started to hold forth. 'Back there in the city,' he said, 'people don't behave the way you people do here. They convert words into power; organized, aggressive power. We've got to do the same, something really urgent, before death gobbles us all up.'

One of the older people curled his lips into a disapproving leer. 'And what do you suggest we do?' he asked, looking up at the sky and then down at the ground. 'You should realize,' he went on before the young man had the slightest chance of replying, 'no one can stand up to the government. We have to make use of our common sense and figure out what we can do.'

'When drought comes,' the young man went on nervily, 'you spend an entire year asleep. When it doesn't, you send letters and petitions. That's it! Al-Tiba will never survive that way!'

'Listen, my boy!' the young man's father retorted, 'Al-Tiba will survive. There have been many bad years like this one before. People have made it through and carried on with their lives. Al-Tiba's still here!'

'When you're living in conditions like these,' the young man said sarcastically, 'there's no real difference between living and dying! Just take a look at the soil, the trees and the livestock. Look at the expressions on people's faces. Everything dying. Another year like this one, and there'll be nothing left!'

This conversation could have gone even further. However, at

this point some guests who had arrived that afternoon came into the guesthouse. With that the whole atmosphere changed.

That afternoon towards the end of summer, four guests arrived. They were brought out by some of the village children who had moved to the city and were now friends of theirs. They arrived in two cars: one a jeep and the other a small, grey Volkswagen. People from al-Tiba, those who actually live there or those who have moved on, are noted for their sensitivity and gentleness. They know how to lick their wounds in silence; it is amazing how they manage to keep their sorrow and troubles to themselves, so much so in fact that many people do not understand them and fail to grasp their real feelings. On their own they will discuss any number of problems and difficulties. But let guests arrive, and all such things are put to one side while they adopt a totally different mode of speaking. This is how the old people differ so markedly from the younger ones. The former are used to keeping their feelings to themselves and to waiting for the appropriate moment before expressing their feelings in public. The latter on the other hand seem to be afflicted by a kind of fever which makes them incapable of keeping their innermost thoughts and feelings to themselves. In seasons such as this one that is so even more than usual.

As a result some people wanted to discuss things for one last time, even though it was in front of guests. Many people in al-Tiba had waited so long for their children to come home from the city that their patience had run out. For one last time they were eager to discuss the prospects for the dam: when was it going to be built, and what were they supposed to do to get the whole thing started. But even they could not wait any longer than they had done already. For many years past they had been patient and endured their hardships in silence, but no more. From now on, they would be resorting to new methods of convincing officials back there in the city of quite how much power they actually had.

Yes indeed, the people in al-Tiba had been waiting for a long, long time. But on that particular afternoon, when they spotted those two strange vehicles coming into the village, their hopes were completely dashed. Fathers and mothers embraced their returning children, and for just a moment the power of love was stronger than the feelings of reproach. Tears welled up in people's eyes, and a whole host of other emotions came flooding up. As a result, the angry thoughts and words which they had been harbouring for so long receded into the background. In their place came feelings of love and cordial words of welcome. This was, of course, the first time the guests had seen al-Tiba, and so as far as they were concerned, nothing seemed out of the ordinary. They were not able to detect that internal malady brought on by sheer dessication. When they found themselves welcomed with such broad smiles, they felt warm inside and even managed to envy these rustic people the contentment which they so obviously possessed!

This was the way many matters were postponed until later. Other things were given priority. The items which the village children had brought back with them from the city were carefully distributed. Some of the older people took others aside and counselled them to behave prudently. They asked the younger people to display the customary respect towards guests by not stirring up troubles or grievances.

'These guests'll only be here for a day or so,' they all told themselves, 'and then they'll be leaving. Once they've gone, we'll be able to give these recalcitrant children of ours a piece of our minds. All they're good for is sending out necessities when drought sets in. Anyone would think al-Tiba had turned into a refuge for the poor and needy and was going to stay that way!'

There had been a good deal of talk about the water which would be available in abundance throughout the year, of fish which would be placed in the reservoir and of canals which would extend for great distances. But that was all over now. A few isolated phrases would do the rounds every few years, but even then it was only out of a sense of pity or sorrow for this village which day by day was gradually dying.

This was the way things went during the first few hours the guests were there; people reacted just as has been described. The village children who had come home sensed immediately that things had changed for the worse. Life in the village had now become so harsh that it was almost inconceivable. They noticed the changes which had made an impact on every single thing they set their eyes on. It did not take long for them to realize how enormous was the wrong they had done. There was absolutely nothing they could say to express the feelings welling up inside them. And now guests had arrived; they would have to be given special treatment. Even so the village children did not have any illusions about the looks, gestures and even brushes of the hand, all of which pointed to the fact that al-Tiba was boiling over and would soon burst at the seams in one way or another. However to the guests everything looked strange and attractive, and so all these pent-up feelings were put to one side.

When everyone got together in the evening, conversation centred on the subject of hunting; that, after all, was what the guests had come for. As long as that was what the guests wanted, that's the way it would have to be!

At certain times people in al-Tiba would be aggressive and lose their tempers. But when occasion demanded, they could also be patient. They would resort to all possible means to combat hunger and death. Whenever hunting was mentioned as a way of coping with hunger and rescuing whatever was rescuable, one phrase, almost like a password, would spring to everyone's lips: 'Where's 'Assaf?' With no particular fuss people would volunteer to go out for him and bring him in. When things were particularly bad and people sensed they were staring death straight in the face, they would start feeling morose, hungry and aggressive. They would counter these emotions by slipping in a terse phrase which would always be pronounced with a leer, almost like a joke: ''Assaf! That's who we need!'

In order to quash a bitter argument which would already be in full swing and liable to go on for ever, someone would say: 'Go and get 'Assaf! Bring him back, dead or alive!'

Eventually 'Assaf arrived. He walked in looking nervous and testy. Muttering an almost inaudible greeting he took a seat close to the door. By now the people of al-Tiba had grown accustomed to 'Assaf and accepted his crazy behaviour. However they were all vehemently opposed to the idea of allowing him to bring his dog into their evening gatherings and meetings. This decision hurt 'Assaf a great deal, and he countered it with a more vehement and acerbic insistence of his own. Eventually a tacit agreement was struck. 'Assaf was allowed to attend the meetings without being forced to shake anyone's hand; the dog could stay by the door. 'Assaf accepted this arrangement reluctantly, but at all events his contacts with village meetings and get-togethers were so infrequent that people rarely set eyes on him. However, whenever a guest came to the village for hunting, 'Assaf was the very first person to be invited to attend. Now, if 'Assaf disliked meetings, he hated these guests just as much; for the most part he regarded them as insipid and naïve bores. But al-Tiba had taught him its own particular etiquette, and so he was compelled to go out with them and behave cordially. That involved a great deal of effort!

On that particular evening when they brought 'Assaf to the meeting, he could tell that things were not normal. He sat by the door and made his dog do the same. At that point he heard several people urging him to move into the middle. When he declined, one of the people from al-Tiba who had brought the guests out with him got up, made a warm gesture of greeting to 'Assaf, and tried to make him come forward. This went on for a while till one of the village elders suggested that 'Assaf move forward and the dog stay where it was.

Into every person's life there come moments of fulfilment. At the time they remain unappreciated. No one can tell how or when they come, or what forces are at work to make them burst out from the inside. Out they come, though, blowing with all the force of a gale and pouring down like an abrupt shower of rain. They overwhelm everything. And then, no sooner have they come than they are gone, like water seeping away rapidly into dry, sandy soil.

No one can possibly plan for such moments, even if he wished to do so. On this particular occasion 'Assaf had come against his will. He felt himself compelled to stare at some people whom he had never set eyes on before and probably never would again either once they had left al-Tiba. He was feeling pretty annoyed because one of the elders had asked him to leave his dog by the door. But now he found himself thrust into a world of passion, the closest thing imaginable to sheer revelation. No sooner had people started asking him about hunting, how many birds he had caught that day and in general how the season was going, than he felt himself choking. He dearly wished he had never come. Even more, he wanted to get out of this awful meeting. But he knew the people of al-Tiba and was well aware of the gruff feelings of affection they all felt towards him; it was as though a bond hundreds of years old was tying him to everything around him, soil, people, trees and water, a bond which was made even stronger and more forceful whenever a really harsh year like this one came along.

At first he was determined not to say a word. The only replies they got to their questions were a few phrases. But then he began to feel an odd sensation inside him, a peculiar blend of congeniality and defiance. His heart was pounding faster than it normally did in such situations. It was at that moment that he made up his mind to do something he had never done before.

He remembers it very well, as does everybody else who was there at the time. For the first time in his life he plunged into the thick of a dispute. People were forever saying that his life had always been one long struggle, but he had never taken on such an issue as this before. The questions were still raining down on him, all of them about hunting.

'Hisan!' he yelled defiantly, 'Hisan, come ... come here!' The dog sprang to its feet, slunk over like a snake and settled down at 'Assaf's feet.

The whole thing happened so suddenly. No one anticipated it. For a few moments everyone was too shocked and bewildered to do anything. The village elders who usually called the shots realized that, in calling his dog over to him, 'Assaf's tone of voice had sounded very unusual; it would obviously brook no opposition. They looked at each other helplessly and then at 'Assaf. For the first time ever in their long and eventful lives they saw in 'Assaf's expression a cruel, savage glint. All thought of objecting to the dog's presence vanished quite unconsciously. Instead they all shook their heads regretfully, a gesture which carried with it a certain amount of reproach as well.

'Assaf did not wait. Adjusting his position he stared long and hard at everyone sitting around. A heavy silence filled the air. He stretched his hand out to the dog in a gesture full of tenderness and love and scratched its back more than once.

'So what are your thoughts, you people of al-Tiba?!' he intoned without looking at anyone in particular; it was almost as though he were talking to himself. 'Do you seriously imagine that this year's just like all the other bad years you've gone through in the past? Do you really believe you're going to carry on till the rains come again? Well, let me tell you, anyone who thinks that must be well nigh insane!'

He paused for a moment to take a deep draw from his cigarette. Then he stared at them again. 'I've told you a thousand times, before. Only a short stretch separates us from death, and it consists of the game which we have to preserve till the rains come again. I've told you that hundreds of times, but you'll never listen to me. Instead you get more stupid as the days go by! I've told you all: don't touch the female partridges; they're needed for future years. They're all we have left. I've told you: don't waste ammunition, and don't scare the birds. Then they'll come to you instead of you having to go out to them. But do you listen? No! What do you do? Day after day you get more and more stubborn. Didn't I tell you all just to take two or three donkey-loads of water, put them into some of the cisterns close to the village and hang around till the birds come? You all smiled sarcastically, didn't you? Oh, you all said, 'Assaf's gone off his rocker again; fancy expecting us to waste the little water we have left by sprinkling it around in the desert! And now here you are bringing these city types out here and putting on a big display of generosity and kindness. I suppose you'll be expecting good old 'Assaf to take them out hunting and let them join in as well! What are they, or anyone else for that matter, supposed to hunt now that you have filled the heavens with the sound of gunshots being fired crazily into the air. Every bird in the sky and every beast on the ground has been listening to that row for ages now; there's been no stopping you!'

He threw up his hands in a despairing gesture and then looked straight at the guests.

'Gentlemen,' he went on in a different tone of voice, 'in the old days partridges used to come right up to the door. Gazelles and rabbits were to be seen all across the plain. The ravines were so full of turtledoves that even 'Assaf could not make up his mind which one to go to first. That's the way things used to be. But the people of al-Tiba did not preserve this bounty. Instead they showed any bastard from thousands of miles around how to get here. Excuse me. I am not referring to the present company, of course! You are our honoured guests. I mean other hunters who come from all over the place, as though al-Tiba's the only hunting spot in existence. All these people want to do is kill animals. They used to kill absolutely everything in sight. They'd shoot female partridges before the male ones because the males used to panic and fly away, and that scared them a lot. When they had got their courage back, the female birds would take to the air and the hunters would shoot them down. They did precisely the same thing with gazelles, rabbits and other species. They came back to the village laden with game, but that was not enough for them. They had to tell their friends and their friends' friends all the way down to the proverbial tenth generation. They used to bring all sorts of unbelievable weaponry out with them, things which could blast rocks apart. So year by year al-Tiba was gradually but relentlessly despoiled. And now here you are, expecting 'Assaf to produce birds, animals and God knows what else out of thin air. Tell me, what's 'Assaf supposed to do? Is he supposed to be some kind of Christ? Does he lay and hatch the eggs, or what?'

Once again he stretched out his hand and rested it on the dog's back. Silence reigned over the entire assembly. They all looked astonished as he stared at them.

'Game was not invented for the rich and those who are motivated purely by greed. It was created for the poor, people who cannot earn their own daily bread. 'Assaf has spent his entire life in the desert and yet even in good seasons he has only hunted just enough to fill his dog's stomach and his own. When dry seasons come, it's fair enough to hunt so that people won't die on the streets. That's like using wheat bread instead of barley bread. But there's something which people in al-Tiba and in every other town and village I know simply don't realize: these days man has acquired a temperament of truly evil proportions, something not even wolves or other similar species possess. And that's why we're facing hunger today. Tomorrow's hunger will be a lot worse and more difficult to cope with. I can see it all just as clearly as I see all of you now. I'm even more worried about tomorrow than today. We've only ourselves to blame; we have done it all with our own hands!'

'Assaf now started fidgeting rudely to show how desperate he felt about the situation and how eager he was to get up and leave. The things he had said had created a tense atmosphere; this was particularly the case for the people of al-Tiba who had their guests to deal with. There was an unusual amount of movement, both rapid and subtle; it managed to express that gentle element of protest which would normally accompany a grudging and implicit acknowledgement that what this madman had been saying was absolutely true. No one could deny or disavow it. What he had said needed to be said!

Na'im was one of those who had brought the guests out from the city. He had been telling them a great deal about the hunting in al-Tiba and about 'Assaf and his proverbial gift for hunting. He had also told them about his odd moods. It was now his task to try to lessen the impact of what 'Assaf had had to say.

'You're absolutely right, 'Assaf,' he said. 'But you are well aware of that crazy streak which lingers in a hunter's heart ...'

Now one of the guests joined in. 'There's no hunting to be had anywhere,' he said in a tone of resignation, almost as though he were defending himself. 'It's not just al-Tiba.'

'Who said that al-Tiba was the only place with madmen?' 'Assaf retorted with a sarcastic guffaw, almost as though this were one of the very few instances in his entire life when he had been amused. 'This particular madness is to be found all over the place,' he went on, just to make sure that his statement was clearly understood. 'Even if those new weapons were made by lunatics far away, who ever said they had to come out here and be used for hunting? They kill everything in sight! There's nothing left!'

Once again his tone became sarcastic. 'It's all very well for other parts of the country. They're well provided with water and greenery and can get whatever they need without a lot of effort. Key figures in the government and army hail from those places! But al-Tiba's just a poor village. If it rains, the village can feed itself. If there's drought, people die of starvation!'

Another change of tone. 'In olden times long, long ago, we could face starvation and stand a chance of winning. In those days birds used to come in from the desert and other animals could be found close to the village. We used to keep up the fight by eating rats and jerboas. But these days there's nothing left. If things go on like this much longer, the only things left in al-Tiba will be owls and bats!'

Another guest chipped in. 'I've heard they're going to build a dam for you,' he said coyly, attempting to visualize how al-Tiba might be. 'This dam's supposed to irrigate a wide area. Isn't that so?'

'We've all been hearing the same things as you,' one of the elders commented. 'The difference is that we've been hearing it for ages. Officials in the city have been telling us such things but who knows if it will ever happen!'

The man gave a sarcastic laugh and shook his head in despair. 'Just forget about the village's problems,' the Mukhtar of the Eastern Sector said. 'The important thing is to arrange a proper hunting expedition. These good people won't forget al-Tiba when they go back. They'll spare no effort in persuading government officials to build the dam quickly!'

With that the whole atmosphere suddenly changed. One of the company lunged in 'Assaf's direction and kissed him on the top of his head. 'You'll be leading the expedition, Butrus,' he said enticingly. 'Tomorrow we'll bring back lots of game!'

'You'd better do a lot of hunting,' one of the elders joked. 'Hunting alone isn't going to stop al-Tiba from dying!'

The entire assembly, including the guests, gathered round 'Assaf and started making preparations for the next day's expedition.

'There's no point going after quail,' 'Assaf said to reconfirm the previous evening's understandings. 'We'd come back empty-handed. They've been killed off for a thousand kilometres all around. The partridges will probably fly away too; by now they're scared of men or ghosts. They'll fly a long way away. That's why we'll have to go as far out as possible. As long as we've got cars, each group can serve as a beating party for the other.' He paused for a moment and looked around. It was still pitch dark. All you could see were flashes from people's eyes and the occasional glow of a cigarette when someone took a puff.

'Well,' said 'Assaf as he began to move, 'now it's up to you! Good luck, and use your common sense!' The twilight air was filled with gentle breezes which left in their wake a wonderful lingering coolness. The men were all squeezed into two cars. They preferred to let the time pass in silent contemplation. Once in a while there would be some terse chatter, but for the most part their only purpose was to break the barrier of silence and boredom, to build up some sense of collective enthusiasm for this venture, or above all to bolster their fondest hopes. 'Assaf was sitting in the front jeep. He remained silent and gave only brief replies to questions directed at him. All he would say was: 'Be patient! You'll see soon enough!'

'Assaf was the one who knew the way. From time to time he would give precise directions to the driver:

'Right!' 'Left!' 'Left again!'

The driver would respond to these commands immediately. There would be no objections. Once in a while he would make a mistake. Instead of turning to the left as 'Assaf had instructed, he would give a vigorous pull on the wheel and head off to the right. The car in the rear was fairly far behind them so as to stay out of the way of the thick dust-cloud which flew up from the jeep's wheels. For them each one of these twists and turns came as a surprise. At once their hopes were roused about the promised game; they were expecting something to happen at any moment. However 'Assaf was the one completely familiar with the terrain, and he remained absolutely calm. One of the passengers in the back seat of the jeep was bold enough to ask 'Assaf if it was time to get the guns ready.

'Patience is a virtue ...' 'Assaf replied testily. 'Just wait!'

'Mightn't we come across a rabbit or wolf somewhere?'

'Are there any rabbits left?'

'I thought this was rabbit country.'

'Then stop thinking!'

Once again conversation ground to a halt. The roar of the jeep's engine was the only audible sound; the only thing to be seen was the area illuminated by the jeep's headlights. They were driving along one of the few tracks which the people of al-Tiba would use to take their guests so far into the desert. With every mile they covered the nature of the terrain and air changed.

Geologically speaking, the area round al-Tiba itself was quite varied. It started with some black rock formations which almost served as al-Tiba's boundary markers on this side; then there were some earth dunes interspersed with limestone outcrops, followed by fertile soil of considerable variety. In such terrain the small bits of rock are on the same level as the soil and, with a few minor variations, stay that way for a long stretch until they are interrupted by the valley. In winter this valley turns into a watercourse for streams swollen by the rain; at such times people can hardly cross it. It curves away abruptly towards the West for about a mile or two and then the desert starts to appear.

The desert's aspect is tentative at first, almost as though it had been fashioned in a hurry. The ground features are very similar to those of the surrounding areas. But then bit by bit the soil starts to change until it turns into a single, repetitive pattern, looking for all the world like the palm of a person's hand with a few isolated wrinkles. From time to time sand dunes appear and then vanish.

Now the desert proper started. 'People sitting by the windows can start loading their guns now,' said 'Assaf clearly.

The response was automatic and fervent. The sound of rifles being loaded with bullets could be heard. 'Assaf turned round and spoke to the man who was sitting in the middle of the back seat:

'When we get to the real hunting area, you'll sit where I am ... here!'

Na'im, who was driving the jeep, felt distinctly uneasy at the thought of 'Assaf leaving them to their own devices in such a fearsome desert. 'What about you, 'Assaf?' he asked.

'Assaf allowed himself a smile, the first time he had done so since they had started out. He looked at the driver and then at the men sitting in the back seat. The first light of dawn was gradually seeping through and penetrating to the inside of the jeep. He stared at them for a moment.

'My dog and I'll be on foot,' he said. 'You'll be in the car.'

'How are we supposed to hunt?' asked one of the three men in the back seat.

'The car'll do it for you!' 'Assaf replied sarcastically.

He realized that no one had understood. 'Hunters have been out here for years chasing birds and wearing them out,' he went on in a different tone of voice. 'Now the birds are scared of absolutely everything. The only way to hunt them is in cars.' He paused for a moment and looked around. 'When you spot a covey of quail or partridges,' he went on with yet another change of tone, 'you must go for them at full speed. You can get a few birds before they all start flying and get too far away.'

'But what about you, 'Assaf?' asked Na'im who was allowing the steering-wheel to shudder in his hands as he clasped his rifle.

'Assaf gave him an encouraging look. 'Don't worry,' he replied, 'my dog and I will be on foot. The birds which get away from you will head in my direction and come quite close. They'll be for me!'

The party proceeded a bit further. Finally 'Assaf sensed that they had reached the right spot. He took a long, panoramic glance at the horizon to make quite sure and then gestured with his hand, a movement which was accompanied by some incomprehensible mumbling noises. All this was to make Na'im stop the jeep. He did just that, so abruptly in fact that everyone expected a surprise: maybe 'Assaf had already spotted some game, or something like that. Instead 'Assaf simply opened the door and signalled to his dog to get out.

'We should stay in a circle formation,' he stated quite calmly, as though delivering a sermon. 'It can expand or contract, but it should still be a circle. The birds won't go far away. All you have to do is learn how to help each other. The people in the second car have to understand that too.'

In a little while the second car arrived and came to a gentle halt alongside the jeep. 'Assaf was not about to leave anything to chance.

'The dog and I will be on foot,' he shouted. 'Each one of you should hunt for birds in a particular direction. The quail won't be frightened at this time of day. They don't take off in a hurry; you can drive a car right into the middle of the covey without them flying away. If you're real hunters, you'll get a good catch!'

The next words seemed almost addressed to himself. 'As far as I can tell, no one's been here for a good while. If-the birds haven't been shot at too much, they won't panic and fly away. Then the hunting'll be good.'

'You should stay with us, Abu Layla!' suggested one of the men from al-Tiba. 'The car's big enough for all of us; it can do the thing in stages.'

'No, it's better for me to be on foot ... ' He paused for a second. 'Our friend will sit in the front seat here,' he went on, pointing to the man who had been sitting in the back.

A brief period of silence now followed. But 'Assaf did not want any more discussion of the matter. 'It's better for you to be in cars and to help each other,' he went on. 'Each car can scare up birds for the other one. I'll be on foot; that's the hunting technique I know best!'

For several minutes there was an increasing round of clarifications, particularly from the people of al-Tiba who were accompanying the guests. 'Assaf also participated in the process. His contributions were short, but very clear and to the point. Finally everything was agreed. The cars were on the point of moving off, each one in its own direction. But before they did, Na'im handed 'Assaf an ammunition cartridge and put out the headlights.

With that the hunt began! The fresh morning air lent the whole of creation an awesome softness; the sensation stimulated a shudder of sheer pleasure, a feeling of delight which immediately penetrated to the very bone marrow. The vast, limitless expanse created its own special sense of awe, one which only occurred at particular moments within nature's domain and in very unusual circumstances. Grey-coloured in the dawn light, the desert stretched away into the distance;

only the sea itself could rival the sight. Feelings of smallness and finality came to the fore and then once again of assimilation, the kind which only makes itself known when the wind is blowing hard and rain pours down in an apparently never-ending deluge. The all-enveloping sense of darkness made all creatures, especially human beings, feel puny and transient. This feeling is always stronger in the desert than anywhere else; to an inconceivable extent one gets the feeling of being abandoned and alone. This loneliness triggers sensations of fear, terror and anticipation, a desire to hide, to shout out, to be united with something or other, not to mention a thousand other feelings which cannot be described in words.

In the desert a person can feel completely alone even when he is with other people. He will have this inkling that he is facing an enemy a thousand times more powerful than himself. This particular foe cannot be resisted. There is no choice; one either has to come to an understanding with him, try to outsmart him, or else accept his terms.

All these feelings flooded into the hunters' minds as they confronted this universe for the first time. Even those among them who had an overwhelming desire to hunt under any circumstances now began to feel scared. Lurking deep down inside them were veiled misgivings: 'What happens if we get lost? What if the cars get bogged down in those blasted raging sands? Why couldn't those birds find somewhere else to live besides this desolate spot?'

Man may have all the power in the world; within himself he may have at the ready all the defiance he feels he needs. But in circumstances like these he shrinks in size. He begins to wish he had shown more sense and never embarked on such a trial. Even hunting in such a wild and desolate spot has a particular flavour of its own. The whole thing turns into something like an escapade. The real goal is to prove his own abilities to himself and corroborate his existence, not merely to provide the usual pleasures of hunting, the wait followed by the final pounce. In the desert man acquires qualities which come bursting out from within him: modesty, an attempt at self-perception, and patience. He stares around him in awe, helplessly questioning everything he sees. But when coveys of quail start taking to the air like bombs exploding underfoot, then man turns into an entirely different creature. Suddenly he turns into a complete idiot, chasing his own shadow, struggling with his own self and trying to put an end to it before turning to something else. All fear and terror vanish immediately. In a trice he is turned into a particular brand of wild animal. When that moment is over and time has elapsed, he will look back on the whole episode with a kind of satisfaction bordering on envy. 'Did I really undertake such a venture?' he will ask himself boastfully. 'Did I emerge from it safe and sound? Can anything rival hunting in the desert?'

And so the trip began. All attempts at recovering those moments fail dismally in the face of this towering, all-pervasive kingdom of nature. The two cars moved off. Suddenly everyone felt scared. None of the seven men crammed inside could think of anything intelligent to say; they could not even keep a grip on their own behaviour.

The cars moved slowly at first and in no particular direction. In each car the driver kept looking at the people around him and at the other car. Both of them were afraid and had misgivings about what might happen. There were even moments when they regretted ever agreeing to go on a hunting trip to a spot like this. The two cars were not very far apart, no more than a couple of hundred metres, but even so everyone felt helpless as they looked back across the desert and saw 'Assaf's image getting further away and fainter by the second. His dog was still visible, but then even it started to get smaller and smaller and finally disappeared!

All of a sudden there came one of those wild and crazy moments: without any warning a whole covey of quail took to the air. In the pre-dawn gloom they looked like phantoms, and the loud noise they made as they took off lingered for quite a while. This was not one of those sounds which affects just your ears and eyes; this one penetrated to your very core. A few random and futile shots were fired one after another, but the only result was a trail of blue smoke which dissipated slowly on the morning breeze.

This then was the first surprise. It was the hunters in the jeep who had come across the covey. Each one of them now felt a sense of failure and a new resolve. And of course they all immediately came up with a battery of excuses to explain their failure. The hunters in the second car just looked on feeling jealous and thoroughly exasperated; deep down they made a resolution not to repeat such a dreadful mistake. The tame excuses which the men in the jeep had to offer for their failure were countered by curses and challenges from the men in the other vehicle. This was their first encounter. As happens with failures in all walks of life, this one engendered a determination akin to sheer irresponsibility. Hardly had the covey of quail disappeared from view on the horizon before the two cars were speeding off again. The whole group were now possessed by a tentative but perceptible longing for adventure. Guns were hung out of the car windows a little further. Eyes were flashing with an anger born of frustration.

The men from al-Tiba had encountered many types of hunter. As a result they always showed the greatest care and discretion in the designations they used to evaluate other hunters. But by now they were sure of one thing: anyone who knew so little about the desert that they could not even spot that first flight of birds would certainly be a total failure on their first hunting trip. Of course, the men from al-Tiba did not say as much directly, but they themselves were convinced. The majority of guests would come out making great claims for their prowess as hunters; they would go on about all the birds they had hunted and the places to which they had been. However experience would prove otherwise. They would often complain that the mountains around al-Tiba were rougher than any they had ever seen, and that al-Tiba's quail were unbelievably perverse. They would say things like this while climbing the mountains. When they went on the turtledove trail and returned with a small bag, they would come up with a whole series of unbelievable excuses which were almost puerile.

But now, here they all were in the broad expanse of the desert. Right before their eyes all these birds were taking flight and getting them all excited. Yet they could not think up any lies to explain how they had failed to catch any. But that's the way it is with hunters: first the headlong rush to meet the challenge, followed by excuses, and lastly unadulterated lies.

At that moment a second covey took flight just as the first had earlier on. The jeep had tackled a number of them by now; some had flown around the car itself, almost as though they had been inside a cage and then suddenly released. Now it was the second car's turn to face a flock of birds; this one may even have been somewhat bigger than the first. The men in the second car may have had better excuses: the windows in the car were smaller, and it was almost impossible to manoeuvre easily. On the other hand the men in the jeep found it harder to justify their failure.

The two cars kept looking for a circular pattern to follow. The men inside each vehicle began to feel genuinely distressed; they felt almost ashamed and even scared at times. A whole hour went by and dozens of coveys took flight, but the men in the Volkswagen only managed to shoot down three birds while the men in the jeep bagged two. Everyone was anxious to widen the circle. Then they could cover more terrain and return with a larger bag. They were all feeling really glum. They were well aware that, now that they had filled the sky with so much wild shooting for so long, 'Assaf would make fun of them if they returned with their present bag. This feeling was not restricted to the men in one car or to just one hunter either; it was a silent and implicit assumption. No one could bring themselves to say it out loud, but everyone was acting under its impulse. When anyone suggested they go to this place or that, there would be no objections. Everyone was worried, especially since everyone assumed 'Assaf had bagged hundreds of birds by now.

These feelings certainly held a powerful, if cryptic, sway over them all. Even so, from time to time other sensations made themselves felt as well: in particular, fear of the desert itself and the thought of wandering around in this cruel sea with no beginning and no end!

The sun rose high in the sky, and with it up came the heat and dust. Everybody felt the need to regroup, however cruel and bitter the experience might prove to be in the light of their dismal failure as hunters. This was all the more so since 'Assaf had told them that, as the day proceeds, quail move away in search of water and food in faraway places. Hunting in the daytime, he had assured them, was difficult and well nigh pointless.

And so, through some unseen and halting process, the two cars gradually began to move towards the centre of the circle. Of course, there may be circles anywhere in the world and they will all have centres. But from this particular point of view the desert is a living hell. Every single atom seems like a circle, and everywhere is the central point. Even so the men from al-Tiba knew the wind direction. They remembered that, when they had started, the wind had been blowing from the West. That was how they gradually narrowed the circle. After a whole hour of detailed searching with look-outs, the men in the jeep spotted a blue-black figure in the distance.

'There's 'Assaf,' said one of the men from al-Tiba without hesitation. 'It's 'Assaf!'

There was a huge feeling of relief. Without question or delay the car headed in that direction, and a few minutes later the second car arrived too.

'Assaf lay there stretched out on the sand. His dog was close by and his rifle was laid down beside him as though it were no concern of his. He was playing with the sand, and a trace of a smile could be seen on his face. The birds he had shot were piled in a small mound alongside him with the beaks all pointing neatly in the same direction.

When they spotted the mound of birds he had shot, they were all genuinely thunderstruck. What a pile! From their point of view, the whole thing, the sheer number of them, it was utterly impossible. When they brought their bag out of the two cars, 'Assaf looked at them in amazement; actually it came closer to sheer disbelief. However he managed to keep his feelings under control.

'Hunting from a car requires a lot of practice,' he said in a paternal tone to lessen their sense of failure. 'The coveys which flew away from you came straight towards me here!'

One of the guests asked him how many birds he had taken. 'About twenty,' he replied offhandedly. 'I didn't bother to count.'

He did not ask them how many they had bagged. He was

more concerned to know whether they had encountered a large number of coveys or not, whether they had been close or far away, and whether they had been hit on the ground or had flown away after the men had arrived.

At this point the hunting trip could have come to an end. Had it been left to the men of al-Tiba or to 'Assaf to decide, they would have suggested heading back to the village. They could have had a rest and eaten something beside a large outcrop of rock which they had passed on the way. Someone might have said that the bag was large enough and that another hunting trip could be organized later. But most of the time things have a habit of turning out in ways you least expect. It may be true that the guests were the ones in charge and making the decisions, but one has also to point out that people in al-Tiba have a very subtle temperament and are never willing to say outright what they really want.

'Assaf broached the topic politely. 'Well,' he said to dismiss any possibility of staying out in the desert, 'that's it for hunting today. We won't find a single covey from now till sunset. Even if we did, it would fly away long before we ever got close. No man on earth will be able to catch anything more.'

The men from al-Tiba exchanged glances with each other and 'Assaf and then looked at their guests. One of the latter made a suggestion which met with immediate approval from the others:

'We can go where 'Assaf suggests. After we've eaten and rested a bit, we can take a short trip before sunset and then head back to al-Tiba.'

They had a rest at the spot in the valley in the shade of the rock, but it was not at all relaxing. The place was humid enough for their taste, but the hot desert winds kept blowing in their faces; from time to time they would blow specks of sand which accumulated in piles on the uneven lower slopes and marked the course of streams during the winter.

As they sat there, everyone was drinking and talking about any number of things. At first 'Assaf said almost nothing. On the few occasions when he did have something to say it was hard to hear him, almost as though he were talking to himself. They asked him about the animals he had hunted and where he had gone to do it.

'What's the point of talking about things from the past,' was his only reply, 'when we can no longer hunt anything at all!'

But they were persistent. They asked him about the greatest day of hunting he had ever been on, how many birds and rabbits he had bagged.

'Don't regard me as some kind of wild animal,' he retorted angrily. 'I'm a human being, just like the rest of you. I feel no enmity towards any creature. If some birds and animals tempt me to hunt them, it's because I feel a need, not simply for pleasure. And, even if it were for pleasure, it would never reach the level of sheer annihilation and destruction. Even when a man desires a woman and longs to squeeze her in his arms for ever, he can only do it within certain bounds. If he's a fool and does something beyond the bounds of human nature, then in one way or another he's finished for sure. But I am 'Assaf. People in al-Tiba only recognize me as someone who wanders around the desert and spends his time chasing birds and animals ... 'Assaf, the great hero. I have no desire to hunt just for the thrill of killing. Only in times of dire need will I hunt more than necessary.'

He wanted to go on and find a better way of saying things, but he could not. As he lay there with his dog close by him, his head was so full of thoughts that he could not keep them in order or put them into words. Even if he had wanted to say something, his words would have come out sounding vague and rude; people might not have understood them properly. By the time he had had another drink and had let it surge inside him, he felt that he could put things better. The others meanwhile were talking away merrily, even though no one had asked them to do so; in any case nothing they were saying made sense. They had all been bragging in that boastful tone which really betrays a pack of lies, something which only educated and citified types have really perfected. More than once, he thought of yelling out loud or giving a sarcastic guffaw, but by then he had already swallowed the things he had intended to say. Instead he stared straight at them and watched their antics.

That day 'Assaf felt more melancholy than he could ever remember feeling before. Something seemed to be weighing down his spirits, and it felt as heavy as a rock. It had always been his practice to bark out orders to novice hunters, to take them along narrow river-beds and lead them through difficult terrain, all this by way of showing them that they still had a long way to go before they had learned what hunting really meant: how they had to behave in a sensible fashion and how to distinguish between birds for hunting and others which should be left alone. In the past he had done all this and with not a little skill at that, although at times the reasoning may have seemed obscure. But on this particular day his mood was one of utter resignation and despair. He was prepared to do whatever the other people wanted.

If only 'Assaf had stood his ground at a particular moment; if only he had emphatically refused, something he normally did when dealing with the frivolous and wayward instincts of young men; if only he had not felt an overwhelming sense of despair and sorrow; if only the drink had not gone straight to their heads on that hot summer day and had such a powerful effect; if only the location had been different; if only these things had been the case, none of the ensuing events would have happened. As it was however, things were determined by some hidden force which had an unbelievably strong effect on them all, even though it was utter madness!

It was still before noon. The party had been resting for more than two hours. For the guests who had come out from the city the time of day had an entirely different impact from that on the people of al-Tiba and those who lived in such locales. For, no sooner had one of them suggested that they start hunting again than all the others joined in, almost as though by prior agreement. 'Assaf gave the people from al-Tiba a quizzical stare, but all he could detect in their expressions was a sense of befuddled resignation. They seemed completely incapable of making any decisions of their own; they were behaving like utter imbeciles and agreeing to any demands these city types cared to make.

'Assaf hesitated, but not for long. He got up and spoke to his dog. 'Experience is the best teacher!' he said in a tone full of defiant sarcasm. 'Animals can learn a number of things and pass them on to their offspring. That's how they manage to defend themselves. So life goes on. But human beings ...'

He guffawed. There were no arguments as he chose a new spot. 'Maybe the birds here haven't been shot at yet,' he said as though to convince even himself. 'Perhaps there are some thorns they can use for shade! Heaven help us though!'

His tone of voice and general demeanour were the same when he reached the place which he thought was suitable for hunting. He stopped the car, let his dog out and then got out himself. This time he did not say a word or offer any advice.

'We'll meet back here in an hour or at the most two,' one of the men of al-Tiba yelled out in a loud voice so as to let everybody know. 'It's a long way back to al-Tiba, and we should get back early ...'

'Assaf gave a nod of agreement and made a circular gesture with his hands. Some of them thought this meant he would stay in the middle of the circle, while others took it to be a farewell wave.

The sun is beating down from the heavens like molten lead. The sand feels hotter than coals. Even the dog yelps as it lifts up its paws; it sounds almost like a call for help or a protest, as though it is being made to walk on sharp thorns or broken glass.

When the two vehicles took off, they trailed a huge cloud of dust behind them which completely enveloped 'Assaf and turned him into a part of the desert itself as it stretched away to infinity. The dog let out a howl of protest. For a while it ran after one of the cars, but then slowly made its way back to its master.

There exist places where nature can be seen in all its unbridled power: in seas and oceans, at the summits of mountains, in the depths of valleys, in the frozen ice-floes, in the darkness of jungles. In all these locales nature gives all sorts of warnings of changes to come. There is an internal charge present which cannot remain the same for long and will inevitably change at any moment. The desert, on the other hand, the mysterious, cruel, savage desert with all its surprises, transcends the normal laws of nature simply in order to corroborate them.

Within an hour the entire scene had been turned upside down. A violent wind blew up, and a huge sandstorm transformed everything. Storms like this would push the sand into dunes in much the same way as winds do with the waves of the sea. The sands rolled over and over just like a bale of fresh cotton or the ashes of burnt paper. No sooner did anyone turn to face this sudden onslaught than both throat and eyes were filled with those tiny, soft grains of sand which managed to feel like cinders falling out of an ever-burning coal fire.

The things that happened on that summer day deep in the desert and yet such a comparatively short distance away from al-Tiba are such that no one can recall them without bursting into tears. The fear which gripped everybody during those tense hours of waiting was so strong and utterly debilitating that no one can remember what happened. The words which people try to use to describe events sound curiously weak and befuddled, with no real meaning to them. The people from al-Tiba knew by instinct how cruel the desert can be; they could tell from the smell in the air, from the harsh glare of the sky, from the storms which came out of the valley and across the plain to al-Tiba. They were all well aware of this, and yet even they could not believe the sheer force of the storm facing them now. They had never seen anything like it in their lives before. Their guests were totally panic-stricken and lost all ability to function; they simply turned into a group of human puppets, weeping and pleading. There was just one thing they wanted: not to die!

When fear reaches its peak, men can no longer act. They should have just stopped where they were and waited. But the cruel sandstorms were in control of everything now, leading them ever onwards. On those few occasions when the men stopped, savage winds came roaring down, bringing burning hot sands. Everyone started yelling in panic; they could all sense death's hand tightening its grip on their necks. But they did not stop. Instead, driven on by natural instincts, they tried to escape from the storm. The jeep managed to keep both its traction and power intact, but the other car was like a blind tortoise which had lost its way and had no idea either of where it was going or when it would die. One of the men from al-Tiba suggested that things were so risky that the two cars should stay close together. At that everyone felt a certain sense of relief. In fact, the driver of the Volkswagen was not satisfied merely staying close to the jeep, but insisted on driving in front of it, and just a few metres at that.

In the desert waiting like this for death to arrive is one thousand times worse than death itself. Here death does not come suddenly or in disguise. There is no question of it appearing quickly and finishing everything off. At first it just bares its teeth and sits there on the car windows. From time to time it may kick up a fuss and scream, buffet you in the face and blow a grain or two of sand into your mouth and eyes. When this bit of fun is over, it will retire for a while and start prowling round like a wolf, waiting for the next round to start. And it is not a long wait. Like smoke it soon rises up quickly and forcefully. The mouth goes dry, and eyes assume an expression of panic. Yet another cruel, nerve-wracking wait begins. The same searing agony is there and the same overwhelming power. There is no going back. Once again it starts pounding on the car windows, loudly and continuously. With all this waiting and waiting, a man dies slowly; a thousand times over he dies. He loses all self-confidence; his will dissipates. He falls, picks himself up again, and then totters. His mouth is full of panic-stricken prayers, although he has no idea of where they have come from. He shouts, but there is no sound. He looks at the faces of his companions, only to see his own. He remembers, he resists, he collapses, he falls. Yet again he dies, and rises again from death. He looks out at the few metres of ground which are visible through the windows. He can feel the sand covering everything. He takes a mouthful of water and holds it in his mouth for as long as possible in the hope of getting more energy to put up some resistance and remain in control. He can no longer talk or swallow the water which in any case has turned into salt and saliva. He longs to shout out, to die once and for all. He wishes the earth would suddenly open up and swallow him. He longs for water and shade. And he waits ...!

In the desert even time assumes its own special meaning. It

turns into tiny atoms; the second, the minute, these represent the whole of time. Then it starts breaking up into infinitesimal parts, just like the desert itself. Like some coarse, soaking wet cord it starts relentlessly tightening its grip on the neck and making incisions, but without ever severing it or simply leaving it as it is. The whole thing turns into a prolonged death, assured, expected yet deferred and forever mocking. Men come to feel as though they are being strangled. The heart-beat gets faster, temperatures start to rise, and people's faces turn a blue colour. No one dares look at anyone else for fear of either cracking up completely or bursting into tears.

The heat comes up from the ground and down from the searing orb of the sun high in the sky. There is not even a single moment to take stock or think. When darkness comes, it makes people feel extremely weak and increases their sense of panic a hundredfold.

It is a long, long wait. But then the wind starts up again and the atmosphere clears. The sun sinks towards the West, although no one notices it sliding its way down as one would at sea. The air is full of sand, but gradually a faint light can be made out. The temperature begins to fall. All day the sun has stayed there high up in the sky like the noose of a gallows hanging over everyone, but now people begin to realize that it is going down.

At times like these any thought of conversation is utterly impossible. The struggles going on inside everyone were so intense and contradictory that anything might happen or indeed its exact opposite; and men might behave in exactly the same way. The heat from the sun, the worst enemy of all, began to seem almost gentle and radiant as the huge orb began its descent towards the horizon. The brilliant glare which had enveloped everything during the daytime now became a dream to be forgotten along with the gradual onset of darkness. The winds which in daytime would define direction and lead men to a specific location were transformed in the early darkness of evening into a few random blasts of air accompanied by a wailing sound.

So this is death, each one of them told himself, death and nothing else. In moments of absolute despair such as these, man accepts anything, even death itself; he wills it to come in a flash, complete and terminal. But this situation was not like that. What was happening in this case was a harsh exposure, a stripping away of everything, a process of destruction which gradually split cells apart with a cruelty akin to the hunger of a wild animal. Only the desert at night-time could come up with such a death as this, while the winds continued their never-ending rampage.

Here then is man, that weak and transient creature, faced with a crushing force which neither destroys him nor leaves him to his own devices!

'God help you, 'Assaf!' said one of the men from al-Tiba, his voice choking.

'That's right,' said the man sitting in 'Assaf's place next to the driver, 'where's 'Assaf?'

Once again words simply dissipated in people's mouths. Silence reigned, but it was nevertheless that particular kind of echoing silence that is no silence at all; at every moment and in every place it bursts at the seams. The sound of its moaning can be sensed through every pore of the body.

Then came the moment – no one could say with any certainty when it happened or how much time had passed – the wind started dying down. Gradually the sandstorm abated, although the sky was still wrapped in its heavy and overbearing black mantle. The driver started switching the car lights on and off, and that was regarded as a shrewd and meaningful gesture.

'Someone's bound to see us,' said the man sitting beside him. 'They'll come and rescue us.'

'Why don't you start the car?' suggested the man from al-Tiba who was sitting in the back seat behind the driver. 'Circle round a few times in case 'Assaf spots us or we him. Then we can head towards him or vice versa!'

No questions were asked, nor was there any argument. The car was started and began circling like a tethered animal. Once in a while the driver would turn the lights on in case something happened or a rescue team showed up.

'If we find 'Assaf,' the man from al-Tiba said, 'he'll be able to rescue us. He'll have no trouble taking us all back to al-Tiba. But, if we don't find him ...'

He fell silent. People looked at him, but said nothing. The darkness had already triggered a new type of fear, and any notion that they were about to be rescued sounded like the beating of a sickly heart. As a result, these words echoed around the inside of the car like a warning of impending doom!

It was late in the afternoon of the following day that three cars reached the spot. One of them belonged to the Desert Corps. They came across the two cars and found most of the men half dead. Many of them were unconscious, and the others were in a state of total exhaustion. The Volkswagen had sunk up to its back axle in the sand and was so completely stuck that it could not be moved. The jeep had obviously tried to pull it out with a tow-rope, but it had snapped in several places. The entire water supply had been exhausted; all that remained was an empty water container full of sand. The people who found them said that in less than an hour everyone in the two cars would have been dead. They sprinkled water on their faces and started talking to them, but none of the seven men could utter a single clear word. The best they could do was to make animal-like noises. Two of them started crying; one of the two was from al-Tiba. It was impossible to find out why they were crying; was it simply the relief of being rescued, or was there some other reason?

A few minutes passed. The search party kept asking questions about 'Assaf, but there was no reply. At that the commander of the military vehicle decided to act.

'The rest of you stay here,' he said in a tone which brooked no argument. 'Whatever you do, don't go anywhere. We'll find 'Assaf.'

'He has to be somewhere close,' one of the men from the Desert Corps said to reassure everybody. 'We'll find him!'

With that, the Mukhtar of the Eastern Sector took a deft leap and sprang on to the pick-up truck. No one noticed him as he took up a secure position close to the cabin and clung to the front railing.

With its bluish yellow hues the desert stretched away into

the distance like some never-ending circle with no horizon. As the car sped away with a sudden roar, the guest who had been crying let out a yell and started running after it. He fell to the ground and started groaning. After a while they picked him up, carried him back to the car and gave him some drops of water. He could not stop crying. Eventually he covered his head and started sobbing uncontrollably. This went on for some time.

The main group had to wait. They were still hopeful that 'Assaf would be found. For the most part silence was the best way they could find to express their feelings, but still there were no answers to the questions asked by the men who had come out from al-Tiba on the search party. Actually every expression, every gesture, not to mention their parched and split lips, provided all the answers that were needed. Tears were shed. Everyone stopped talking and instead started staring in every possible direction in the hope of spotting a human form. A single hope lodged like a cool breeze in everyone's heart. Undreamed of supplications of all types kept being raised to the heavens, muttered under the breath like a prayer: please let 'Assaf be alive; let them find him!

During this whole agonizing period the men who were left behind to wait kept seeing thousands of images flashing before their eyes. Some of them seemed jumbled but still interconnected, almost like a dream. But by far the clearest and most forceful picture was that of 'Assaf coming back to the village with dozens of birds and distributing them with unerring skill. Each of them had special memories of him ripping his clothes and shoes in particular places, collecting up the empty shells from the novice hunters, checking them carefully, then preparing them for use the next day and making sure they were powerful enough; how he would eventually dispense with shells made out of reinforced paper and substitute brass ones; how he used to keep some of these shells in a small leather pouch next to his chest, and what a bright flash they would produce when he used them – something he always insisted on – to kill wild animals and nothing else.

Throughout this dire period of waiting these images and dozens of others like them kept running through people's minds like one long tape-recording. Everyone felt sure the earth would open up at any moment and 'Assaf would burst out just like one of his own shots. The people of al-Tiba were quite used to the idea of 'Assaf staying away for two days or even three. Sometimes the snow would cut him off or else the valley might be flooded. By now they were inured to such things and had got used to almost anything he did. That was why they were completely convinced of one thing: 'Assaf would come bursting on to the scene at any moment. The car would come back, and the men inside would imagine that they had failed; they would be feeling very sad. But there he would be in the midst of them all, talking in that strange way of his and using incomprehensible sounds as he talked about yesterday's winds, the wildness of nature and the treachery of the desert. Inevitably he would finish by saying that man is more powerful than nature; he knows how to keep it under control and even trick it!

Thoughts and images fused together. As the sun sank slowly towards the horizon, the fresh winds that were blowing engendered a sense of hope which grew with every passing moment and at the same time a despair which was even more powerful. In this surge of emotion everyone was looking around. The silence was all-pervasive. And then came the sudden ringing shout: 'There's the truck!'

The waiting was more unbearable than anything which had happened up to now; the sheer torture was the worst thing they had been through in their entire lives. No one stayed where they were, even those who were utterly exhausted. The men with wet rags around their heads felt a powerful challenge within them. Those who could not get up and run towards the car sat up to watch 'Assaf get out of the truck.

The expressions on the faces of the men looking down from the roof of the truck were harsh and unequivocal. As it approached and drew to a halt, there were just a few moments when people thought that they had not found 'Assaf; the sands had simply covered him up and swallowed him without leaving a single trace. But then the Mukhtar who was still clinging to the front railing and shaking it nervously, gave a yell and pointed to the back.

He let them all go round the truck and then turned round slowly and stiffly. They all looked, and there they saw 'Assaf.

'He's left us, 'Assaf's gone!' he yelled as though uttering a curse. 'We're the ones who killed him, and the great man's dead!'

It was a gruesome scene, fraught with misery and disbelief beyond comment. There was 'Assaf in the back of the pick-up truck all dried up and rigid. His facial features looked different; on his lips you could see a trace of a smile, a curious blend of pain, despair and mockery. It almost looked as though he were speaking!

The Mukhtar kept screaming and crying uncontrollably. The entire scene was harrowing, draining and totally overwhelming. Stifled sobs could be heard, and many tears were shed. In the desert this all made a loud and mournful noise, almost as if to mark the end of an era!

How can men say nothing for so long? How can they possibly forget all those words and sounds they have been using since the day they were born?

How is all this possible? During the whole two hours it took to get back to the village not a single word was uttered.

The Mukhtar stayed where he was, clinging to the front railing and looking straight in front of him. When the truck stopped at the edge of the village, he managed to stutter out a request, clear enough even so, to the Desert Corps truck commander that everyone should head for his house. Groups of people began to appear; they had been waiting anxiously for news and now they were eager to find out what had happened.

By now it was totally dark. The only way to tell who people were was by their voices.

'Come to my house,' the Mukhtar said. 'We'll gather there.'

'Assaf's body was carried gently inside with a great deal of reverence and awe. Once there it was placed at the front of the guests' quarters. They put a lantern beside his head, and his rifle close to his right hand. All this was done with a quiet efficiency. When they had finished, the Mukhtar gave some mechanical gestures apparently formalized a long time ago which meant that everyone should sit down.

Silence, silence and more silence; that was all. Just a few grief-filled gestures which showed in the quizzical expressions on people's faces. Al-Tiba is a really remarkable and peculiar place. People there never find it easy to reveal their true feelings, and, even if they do have something to say, they do it in their own unique way which few other people can recognize or understand!

No one dared question the Mukhtar. The men from the Desert Corps had helped people carry the body inside, but now they were ready to leave.

'We'll be off now,' their sergeant said. 'We'll get the report ready for submission tomorrow morning.' And with no more ado the truck sped off on its way!

The Mukhtar's eyes were red; he was obviously on edge. Occasionally he would make a meaningless gesture. He kept trying to put the whole terrible nightmare out of his mind; he could not bear the thought of recalling what had happened or of talking about it. In most normal circumstances he had a special knack of directing conversation and talking in a particular way which no one else in al-Tiba could emulate. It was often said that he could pour sugar on death itself and present the most complex and difficult issues in the simplest and most agreeable way. However this occasion left him at a total loss; he seemed both distracted and scared. His hands and face kept twitching nervily. But then the council of al-Tiba was called into session – something which had never happened in such circumstances before. A crushing silence hung over the whole assembly.

'There's 'Assaf!' the Mukhtar screamed at them unprompted and with no forewarning. 'There he is, right in front of you. Look at him!' Without looking round he shook his head in grief. ''Assaf, the great stallion,' he went on in a voice choked by tears, ''Assaf, as bountiful as a cloud-burst of rain; foster-father of the poor, who never got an hour's sleep at night, just so that al-Tiba should go on living and surviving; 'Assaf who loved everyone and killed himself so that people could carry on; 'Assaf, a giant among men. Now he's left you. You're on your own when it comes to fighting the government, the army, locusts and who knows what else. What on earth is going to happen now?!'

His words sank in deep like burning-hot knives. People shook their heads. Tears fell silently to the ground. The Mukhtar noticed this. He was on the point of continuing in the same vein when all of a sudden he had a change of heart; his words became all confused.

'What's the point of words now?' he asked. 'We can go on preaching from now till doomsday. And yet men keep dying day after day, houses collapse on top of us, and we cut down trees with our own hands. But nothing changes!'

'I still can't believe it!' one of the elders butted in, trying to change the subject. 'I can't believe he's dead.'

'Just wait,' the Mukhtar went on. 'You'll see us all fall flat on our faces, one after the other. The sand will swallow us up, and we won't find anyone to pour a drop of water into our mouths.'

He let out a weird laugh which managed to be a blend of mockery, sobbing and searing grief and then continued, 'That's exactly what has happened with this hero of ours.'

'But how did he die?' one of the men asked, his gaze riveted on 'Assaf's body. 'How did it all happen?'

The Mukhtar realized that this new topic would require some movements and gestures, so he changed his position. In any case he wanted to create the appropriate atmosphere in people's minds. 'Listen,' he said. 'We were about to give up the search and come back. We had been everywhere and looked in every single spot where we imagined that 'Assaf might have gone, particularly as the cars had not gone far. Muqbil knows the desert inch by inch. He told us where the usual hunting spots were. As an expert hunter 'Assaf would know these places and could not go any further afield. We searched and searched. More than once the Desert Corps commander got on top of the cabin and looked all around through those binoculars which can pick up a needle from a long way away. But there was nothing. Muqbil looked all around too, and he has eyes like a hawk. He saw nothing either. We were about to go back. We were sure 'Assaf had been buried by the sand and that no one would ever be able to find him. Then Muqbil started stamping on the cabin. The car came to a halt, and the commander got out. Muqbil was staring in one particular direction. At first he seemed a little doubtful, but then his demeanour changed.

'"We must head over to the left," he yelled. "I can see a vulture. I'm not completely sure, but I can see a vulture hovering. As long as it's soaring and swooping like that, there's got to be something there!"

'The commander had the binoculars to his eyes before Muqbil had a chance to finish what he was saying. He looked where Muqbil was pointing. At first he too was doubtful, but then he seemed more sure of himself. He snapped out an order to the driver to head over to the left.

'For a long way the terrain was like the palm of someone's hand; nothing at all on the surface. At first we could not see the vulture, but then we managed to make out a black dot in the distance. It kept soaring and swooping. The first time we spotted it, it disappeared for just a second; we told ourselves it had been an illusion. Muqbil could not see anything. The car was heading in the direction he had indicated, but everywhere was blanketed in silence and the ground was completely devoid of markers of any kind. From a distance the whole thing looked like a mirage.

'But Muqbil stuck to his guns. "That vulture's landed on something," he said confidently. "We'd better get over there and check!"

'The car accelerated. Our eyes were all glued to the spot where he was pointing. As we got closer, we were able to confirm that there was indeed a vulture; from a distance it looked as though it were sitting down like a man. Its jet-black colour made it easy to spot, and, as we came closer, it grew in size. When we were only a few hundred metres away, it flew off. As flashes of its white colouring became visible alongside the black, it took on a huge and menacing appearance.

'With every yard that the truck came closer to the place where the vulture had been the picture that emerged became clearer and more gruesome than any of us had imagined. 'Assaf was buried in the sand, with only his head visible. The dog was crouched over his head, and it was almost completely buried too. And yet in a peculiar way it formed a kind of enclosure around 'Assaf's body and particularly his head; it seemed almost to be embracing him.

'When we finally got there, everything became completely clear. "'Assaf died before the dog," said Muqbil confidently. "Some birds – maybe this vulture or some others – must have sensed it and come to take their pickings. The dog must have fought them off until they killed it. Just look at the congealed blood on the dog's head. The birds must have attacked it with their claws so that they could get at 'Assaf. The dog met its end defending both itself and 'Assaf. It must have died either of thirst or when the birds attacked it ...."

'That said, Muqbil proceeded to remove the sand which had completely enshrouded 'Assaf's body and pulled him out. His water canteen was empty, and he was still clutching his rifle. He must have fallen over and got up again a number of times because his left hand was misshapen and bruised. Luckily for him, he had fallen on his face; but for that, the vulture would have eaten his eyes and mangled his face. When the dog had seen 'Assaf fall, it had stood on top of him. No doubt it had tried to save him somehow, but the storm had been too powerful for the two of them!

'That was how 'Assaf met his end.'

The Mukhtar fell silent and placed his hands under his temples as though he were trying to stop his head from falling or else remembering something. A heavy silence ensued.

'I would have liked to bring the dog back with us,' he added in a completely different tone of voice which sounded as though it were coming from another world. 'The poor creature certainly deserved it. But I didn't dare broach the subject. Somehow it didn't seem appropriate in the circumstances, and no one would have understood. Once we had put the body in the pick-up truck, I stood there for a while staring at the dog. I couldn't take my eyes off it. Just then the commander of the Desert Corps truck butted into my thoughts.

'"Our job isn't over yet," he said in a harsh, nervous tone of voice. "We've still got to get back to the rest of the group."

'When I got up into the truck and stepped over 'Assaf's corpse, I took a closer look at him. The expression on his face was very sad. I do not know how, but I heard 'Assaf's voice speaking to me: "The dog," he was saying, "are you going to leave the dog behind?" With not a little trepidation I went over rapidly to the two soldiers in the front of the truck. I could not bear to look back. I was afraid, afraid of seeing 'Assaf, of hearing those chiding words of his. I became even more afraid when the sun started going down. I thought of all the people waiting for us, of al-Tiba, humanity in general, and heaven knows what other miseries as well.'

'You should have put some earth over the animal so the birds wouldn't eat it,' said one of the village elders in a sorrowful tone of unusual intensity.

'We should have brought it back with us,' the Mukhtar replied testily.

'You can't bring back dead animals,' the elder re torted. 'But the decent thing to do is to cover them with earth.'

The Mukhtar shook his head, obviously suffering from the burden of intense sorrow and regret. He said nothing more.

Now the baker spoke up. 'One of the most incredible features of this world is the relationship between mankind and his surroundings: animals and trees, houses and rivers, even the desert which is never very far from al-Tiba. In a whole variety of circumstances man has connections with them all because they are his salvation. If it weren't for that, 'Assaf would have never gone there. He wanted to save al-Tiba and me in particular: the few loaves of bread which I was able to bake were no longer enough for anyone.'

'It's the same in al-Tiba as everywhere else,' said another man who had not spoken so far. A tear fell from his cheek as he went on: 'The thing which needs to change is man himself.' He fell silent for a moment while he unconsciously wiped the tear from his cheek and then continued. 'If we'd understood what 'Assaf was saying, we would be in better shape now.'

'Well, now he's gone,' said one of the elders, 'and he'll never be back.' He paused for a moment and smiled sadly. He was about to continue, but someone else got there first.

'Most of the time,' this new speaker said, 'things have a habit of coming too late!'

'If all al-Tiba's going to do is wait for rain,' said a youngster whose presence no one had noticed up till now, 'then everyone will die the way 'Assaf has. Maybe it'll be even worse!'

'The worst thing we did to 'Assaf,' said the Mukhtar, 'was to let him fight on his own. Even his dog was better than us. At least it tried to save him. We did absolutely nothing.'

'Abandoning a man is the very worst thing we can do,' one of the men said. 'But a dog ... well, that's just the way things are!' He gave a sigh and then continued. 'I knew 'Assaf wanted to die. One way or another he was bound to kill himself; if not on this trip, then on some other one; if not in the desert, then buried underneath the snowdrifts. You all remember the way he used to live his life: how many times he got lost and how often we had to go out looking for him ...'

He was on the point of continuing, but one of the elders interrupted him.

'People seem to find it odd that we can't distinguish between human beings and animals a lot of the time. Sometimes animals can be better than a lot of human beings. But ever since that dog came to al-Tiba, I've had the uneasy feeling that one day it would kill 'Assaf.'

'It wasn't the dog that killed him,' the Mukhtar interjected angrily. 'We're the ones who killed him.'

'It doesn't matter who killed whom. What matters is that 'Assaf over there can no longer hear us or sense our presence.'

'Don't you believe it!' the Mukhtar retorted angrily. 'He can hear; every single word he can hear. He's taking in everything that's being said here.'

'People of al-Tiba,' said one of the elders, 'don't be even more stupid than necessary. The man's dead. No power on earth can bring him back; only God can do that. If you really want to pay your respects to 'Assaf, then let him rest in peace. Stay with him till morning. We'll carry him out at first light and return him to the earth.'

As the session began, the atmosphere was fraught with a sense of mystery and of defiance too. Never before had al-Tiba felt such a spirit of veneration, prompted perhaps by fear or else by palliatives and postures in the face of death. As a general feeling of awe pervaded the entire assembly, a number of people, including the guests, longed to see the whole thing done differently. However the Mukhtar was not to be dissuaded; his stubborn insistence was as inscrutable as it was firm. His voice was filled with emotion.

'You must stay with us, 'Assaf,' he said nervously, 'then you'll be able to see everything.' With that, he turned his head away. His eyes were closed, and he held his hands up in a gesture with infinite significance. 'You aren't dead. 'Assaf,' he went on as though talking to himself, 'you're still with us.'

'Listen, you people,' said a voice from the back. 'Life and death are in the hands of God. It's all over now!'

''Assaf will never die,' said a young man nervously. 'He's more alive now than all of us put together!'

'Don't blaspheme, young man!' said the elder. 'The angels are hovering above us at this very moment.'

Abu Zaku who built everything in the village, including graves, was the next to speak. He was anxious that everyone should forget their worst forebodings, and decided to try a common-sense approach. 'Listen, folks,' he said, 'morning's still a long way off. Tomorrow we have a grim duty to perform. You can either recite the Quran and talk, or else everyone can go home and come back tomorrow morning.'

'The door's wide open,' said the Mukhtar testily. 'Anyone who wants to leave is free to do so.' He paused for a moment to assess the impact of his comment and then continued. 'For my part, I do not intend to sleep for a single moment. I shall stay awake right alongside 'Assaf here till dawn breaks and we carry him to his grave!'

So began the incredible all-night session, something al-Tiba had never witnessed before. Almost everyone who was there said something. They talked of many things. The guests told stories too, but the people of al-Tiba did not understand them too well. Many, many things were said that night, and all the while 'Assaf lay there enveloped in a shroud with his face uncovered. The light danced on his features and on those of the others present, creating an ambience which was both eerie and awesome. There was a certain manic aspect to the whole thing; not for a single second did anyone there want to stop. The order in which the tales were told was governed by neither logic nor intention. It was just that everyone was gripped by a fervent desire to avoid silence and overcome it at all costs.

They talked about dogs, gazelles and donkeys, about floods in the valley, about the spring drying up, about 'Assaf and humanity in general. Someone was bold enough to recite some verses of poetry. A shepherd was even on the point of playing his flute, but one of the elders snatched it away from him and gave him a frown!

No one can remember exactly what was said or who said it. But whenever al-Tiba indulges in reminiscences and sorrows intrude, on those occasions when conversation turns to the way humans and animals, even trees, meet their death, then the picture of this incredible night invariably comes back to remind people of one thing: the end!

At first the guests had frozen in sheer panic. One of them had even vomited more than once at the sight of the corpse laid out in front of him. But gradually, through that instinctive process, almost akin to a type of catharsis, to which all men have recourse once in a while, they forgot everything or at least kidded themselves that they did. They felt themselves drawn into the dimly-lit rooms to which people of al-Tiba had taken them. There they listened and talked. Every gesture still evoked a sense of uneasiness, even if it was merely adjusting their position to prevent themselves from falling asleep. Abrupt coughs, the tears which welled up however hard one tried, even they created a sense of alarm.

And then came the stories. As the narratives proceeded that night, a sensation of utter grief was created, powerful enough to cling to people's skin and bones. It dug a deep furrow into their hearts which seemed to haemorrhage thereafter whenever al-Tiba recalled these sad events or the conversation turned to the topic of animals or even houses which had fallen down or the all-pervasive dust. As people recalled these stories, everything had its own special aroma which reminded people of sorrows without end.

Some of the Stories from that Remarkable Night

THE FIRST STORY

The years of drought arrived, and with them locusts. Then the strangers came. All this produced a change in people and the nature of life itself. The older people found themselves so overwhelmed by worries and sorrows that many of them felt no compunction about declaring in a loud voice that even death itself was a better fate than the lousy life they were leading at that time.

'The Day of Resurrection will come at any moment,' others said. 'Then life will come to an end.'

This accursed vogue for change brought with it those dreadful cars which looked like tents, cars with angular features and rasping engines. They could take on any terrain however hard; nothing could stand in their way. They would cover large distances at speed and plough through sand as though it were water. If there were any stones in the way, they would simply thrust them aside like a mule kicking stones out of its path. The elders would often suggest that the cars must have had devils hidden somewhere inside them, since no other creature could do the things they did.

The desert animals also developed an instinctive feeling for these changes and started to scare easily. They abandoned the spots where cars would pass by and avoided the watering-holes close to the highway. They made do with as little food as possible. That meant that they could keep out of the way of all this traffic and avoid those crazy moments when human beings were transformed into wild animals somewhat akin to a howling gale.

This is the way life was up to a certain point. However it was rich people and strangers who seemed more inclined than most to indulge in moments of sheer madness. When those devilish spirits took hold of them, they turned into demons. Those who at first refused to use landrovers soon adapted to them. It was then that the elders started warning each other in loud tones that the Day of Resurrection was not something they. had to wait for; they were staring straight at it.

When the wind comes up, it serves as a warning of rain. According to the very same principle things now began to change quickly. The desert was completely transformed. It was crisscrossed with roads. The silence was shattered by the roar of engines. At night the dark expanse was pierced by headlight beams which looked like falling meteors. Places unfrequented by lizards or demons were invaded by human beings from

heaven knows where. Once there, they began opening res-
taurants of a type no one had ever encountered before and
charged exorbitant prices for the things they served, water or
boiled tea. When shepherds stopped there for a short rest,
people would stare at them with a blistering contempt. The
process even affected camels. They were inured to the harshest
conditions imaginable, but with time they too turned into
incredible creatures who were forever being startled by something or other. If the mean looks the strangers gave the
shepherds were not enough to make them move on, then the
fuss and uproar the camels made certainly were.

In the desert talk is endless. It shares with the desert the
same breadth, harshness and almost infinite expansiveness. It
is precisely those features of life which are the topics of
conversation. But on that particular day, late in the afternoon a
little before sunset, something happened which created its own
far-reaching echo and had a rare impact.

Al-'Anzi, the crazyman of the village of al-Jawf, was a
hunter; he knew no other trade. After years of using a bow he
had converted with great difficulty to using a rifle. All the other
hunters had been making fun of him for using such antique
weapons. He bragged that he was a born hunter and could use a
rifle just as well as he had used a bow before. He even relished a
feeling of superiority in being able to bring back the game he
wanted and hunt it wherever he liked.

Some day there will be many people who will write about his
skill and knowledge. Many stories will be told about the
madness of genius. That afternoon just before sunset what
occurred was genuine madness.

He cannot imagine how it was he came to agree to such a
phoney game. It all happened so suddenly, in the wake of one of
those challenges which seem to come right out of the blue.

'Al-'Anzi's better with arrows than rifles!' they all said.

He stared at them all to see if they really meant what they
were saying or if it was just meaningless chatter. He gave a
terse laugh but said nothing. They were well aware that, as far
as he was concerned, their words carried no weight; he was
more self-confident than ever.

'Al-'Anzi's a marksman,' that crafty rogue Abu Ghurayfa

injected into the conversation. 'He never misses!' And with that he paused for a moment and grinned.

Now al-'Anzi realized that something was going to happen. Surprise may well be the enemy of man, as people say, but for al-'Anzi it certainly was far more so than for other men. When Abu Ghurayfa paused, a long, bitter silence ensued. Everyone waited for al-'Anzi to say something.

'Al-'Anzi's a marksman,' Abu Ghurayfa repeated. 'He never misses!'

'And that's when he's on foot. Now, give him a speedy car and...'

He left it hanging just like that, smiling but not saying another word!

That evening they agreed that the bet would be a big one.

'I shall take just one shot,' al-'Anzi said as he accepted the challenge. 'You'll see.'

For the first time ever, al-'Anzi felt tense, exhausted and not a little sad. Will I really win this infernal wager, he asked himself. Will I manage to escape all those looks and sarcastic comments? After a while will I too become like those rich people who own landrovers and move around like locusts looking for gazelles? These thoughts and others were ramming around inside his head, but he dismissed them gruffly. He was sure his shot would not miss. He was even surer that this wager would end up the way others did: the whole thing would soon turn into yet another story to be added to the dozens which people had to tell about him. He was unwilling either to acknowledge or deny the sad feeling he had, but it was undeniably there even though it may have been difficult to pin down.

One landrover set off, then others. Some of them waited for a while before setting out. The rendezvous was to be after sunset at kilometre marker one hundred and sixty. For al-'Anzi everything felt different now. He remembered how in the old days he would move around with his bow and arrows; he could recall the time when he would come back and to which spot. In those days these wagers were a matter between him and himself. But when he started using a rifle, the whole thing became more of a challenge than a mere craving. Even so, there was no difference between the two situations as far as he was concerned: his skill was the most important weapon he had. Using another kind of weapon was no different from hunting some other kind of game.

At several points the driver kept urging the landrover on as though he were on the back of a camel. To al-'Anzi the whole thing was more than he could stand. He regretted making the decision and sank into a rueful silence. Never in his life had he subjected himself to such a foolhardy test. The man sitting in the back seat tried to offer him some help by passing the binoculars, but he brushed them away without a word. He kept scanning the dashboard like a hawk. The car was bouncing up and down like a grasshopper; when the driver changed gear, it sounded like the wind in sandstorm season. All this made him carsick. He felt sure that he would not be able to do things the way he normally did. The rifle shot was smaller than a kernel of grain, and any shaking movement, however small, would spoil everything. He recalled the times in this huge expanse of desert when he used to remove the empty shells from their metal canisters. He would have them strung together on a thread and used to finger each one with an amazing regularity. He used to put down a needle at a range of ten metres. No one else could even see it. They would go up and see if he had hit it. Some clever types would claim that the wind had come along and whisked it off the date pit on which they had originally placed it. Al-'Anzi remembered all these incidents as the landrover bounced up and down. There was just one thing he wanted to be sure of: that the rifle would be firmly wedged against his shoulder where no force on earth could budge it. But with the car bouncing around like this, he became more worried by the minute. He felt both ashamed and alarmed. But for that and the big words he had both heard and spoken the night before, nothing could have stopped him withdrawing from the wager altogether. After all, no one could make him do it. He was not convinced that this was the right way to hunt, but everything had happened so suddenly; no thought or intention had been involved. Now he began to have real doubts about the whole thing, and depression set in. He could feel the dust getting into his eyes and clouding his vision. The man in the back seat kept talking, but all al-'Anzi could make out were muffled sounds which he could just hear but not really understand. And then they would die away suddenly. He was still combing the sky for game; the look in his eyes was one of utter gloom.

He knew all the locations where you could find those sturdy mountain goats. They used to take cover behind the rocks by the lote tree. He would never fire a shot until they had had a chance to take a drink, raise their heads in the air and smell the breeze. He would choose the biggest and strongest animal. When he had had enough of the scene, he would fire his shot to kill instantly.

But, as far as he was concerned, everything was different now. He had no idea when to fire. Would he still be afforded those few transcendental moments, that blend of pleasure and danger? Here he was taking a risk without knowing what the upshot would be.

'Al-'Anzi's not the one hunting this time,' he told himself. 'It's the bedouin who's let himself be corrupted by foreigners. There he is, driving the landrover like a maniac; sometimes he lets it take off, at others it rolls all over the place, and then he lets it go crazy. Occasionally he'll even let the engine die, and then there's silence for just a few seconds.'

The afternoon drew to a close, and the sun started sinking towards the horizon. Moist breezes were in the air. Al-'Anzi filled his lungs, but the same depression still seemed to envelop him on all sides.

'Al-'Anzi won't miss,' he assured himself to give his self-confidence one last boost and stave off the agonies of doubt he was feeling. 'It'll be just like every other time.'

It was a little before sunset, a moment when everything seemed a unity – dust, the vast expanse, the glowing red disc of the sun, moist winds which had suddenly come up and were creating a particular atmosphere which pervaded the whole area – at this very moment al-'Anzi spotted the goat.

'There he is,' he yelled grimly.

The driver gazed listlessly around him to catch a glimpse of this fabled goat which al-'Anzi had talked about. He could not see a thing. He turned the landrover sharply to the right in the hope of getting a better view, but still saw absolutely nothing.

The man in the back tried to hand him the binoculars as a final resource, but al-'Anzi pushed them away with a crushing disdain.

'I can't see a thing.'

'Over there on the left by the hill.'

He veered off to the left at a crazy rate and headed for the spot where al-'Anzi was pointing. He could not see anything at all. Stopping the car, he wiped the dust out of his eyes and looked again closely. When he could still see nothing, he asked the other hunter for the binoculars. Putting them to his eyes and making a sweeping half-circle, he saw the animal in the distance. Starting the engine he sped off again like the wind. It was at that moment that al-'Anzi knew for sure that everything was lost.

The car careered across the desert so fast that it looked like a wounded wolf. It kept bouncing and skidding like a ball. Al-'Anzi clasped his rifle with a grim expression on his face; he had the feeling that everything was shaking and about to come apart. He craved the kind of peace and quiet he had known and experienced for so long; he wanted to feel the sheer pleasure of making a choice and the exquisite moment of taking aim. But now he was losing everything: stability, pleasure and choice.

The noise of the engine, the dust and the terrible carsickness, those were the only things he could feel. The goat kept vanishing like a mirage. The bedouin driver who had been egging the car on all the way now went almost berserk. Odd sounds started coming out of his mouth. Setting himself to challenge the very wind, he kept using the most disgusting language. Al-'Anzi felt utterly sick. His eyes glazed over, and he fell deeper and deeper into a grim silence which came to feel like a heavy rock on top of his chest. Every effort he made to keep control of himself and the others ended in utter failure. He was completely helpless.

A really remarkable chase will only occur once in a lifetime. He had heard a lot about the way landrovers could traverse any kind of terrain, however difficult. But now the car seemed more like a rock rolling downhill out of control. It circled the hill once and then a second time. The goat kept appearing and then vanishing; it seemed to have no idea where to go or how to escape this rifle-fire from all sides. There it was, close at first, then far away; visible, then lost to sight, but always running away from this all-pervasive fire. Al-'Anzi, who used to talk about gazelles as though he were talking about women, found that in this instance he was completely helpless and out of luck. The rifle he was holding felt like a heavy corpse, and he had no idea how to move it or get rid of it.

'This is life's final day!' he told himself.

'Get ready, 'Anzi!' the hunter behind him exclaimed.

At that moment he felt as though someone had stuck an awl in his side. The bet was still on. His final moment of joy was approaching and dwindling with every passing moment. The bedouin kept egging him on like a maniac, almost as though he were the one doing the shooting. He kept accelerating like the wind, yelling and cursing as he went. All this made al-'Anzi lose not only his resolve, but also his strength and even his aim. He bumped his head on the windshield, and the edge of the seat kept digging into his side. The goat meanwhile kept running for all it was worth and turning around in a panic to see if there was any way of getting away from this relentless pursuit.

There came that moment when voices seemed to be battering al-'Anzi from every direction. To him it felt as if someone else's hand raised the rifle and leaned it against his shoulder. In a single moment replete with shouts, wagers and confusion the shot rang out.

The sun was about to set. The car engine had been turned off. Six pairs of eyes were riveted to the spot where the goat had fallen. The bedouin and the other hunter who was to serve as a witness had already got out of the car at a staggering speed. Al-'Anzi meanwhile froze in fear and stayed where he was. Before long however shouts and gestures brought him back to his senses. Everyone urged him to come over and take a look at the dead animal. He got slowly out of the car and walked quietly over to the spot. This time did not feel like any of the others: he was utterly desolated. When he came close and saw the scene, the whole world seemed to narrow in front of his eyes; a veil of darkness suddenly descended. Al-'Anzi, who had looked at a large number of goats in his time, had never seen one like this. It was staring directly at al-'Anzi. Slow, thick tears were falling. Its right leg had been shattered and looked like a piece of old stick. The shot had opened a red-black hole in its left side, and drops of thick, viscous blood were oozing out in a jet-black trickle which presaged an imminent end.

Al-'Anzi could not stand looking at it more than once. He was unable to face the thought of riding back in the landrover. Leaving the rifle in the car he never asked about it again. Thereafter no one heard any more about al-'Anzi. Once again, stories about him began to multiply and diversify; reality and fable became intermingled. But the one which had the widest circulation talked about those tears which had transformed the surface of the desert. Every time conversation turned to this type of hunting in the olden days, people would still feel a burden of sorrow.

THE SECOND STORY

The first day ended in failure. A series of tall stories and the effects of a rapacious imagination had all managed to raise people's hopes, coupled to which had been pagan oaths muttered under panting breath. But the end result of it all had been a miserable day. The few birds lying underfoot and hung along the sides of the car served as a final testimony to the depression which pervaded the entire scene.

It is impossible to recall the sounds as they burst into the night air. Lies and fantasies blended with the agony of defeat. The feeling of frustration was so deep that no one was prepared to listen to anyone else. As the men fell asleep and waited for dawn to come, anger was uppermost in their minds coupled with a healthy dose of sheer faith. Both of these proved to be of greater moment than the comments which kept being bandied about: for example, that shots were only supposed to enter the animal through the head or the left side. The madness and hectic pace of the first day, coupled with dozens of other petty fantasies, had made certain things very clear: the error they had committed had been well nigh a crime; and haste was man's worst enemy. The number of birds taken in non-risky areas had been so great that no one could recall how many!

Of all the hunters he was the one with the greatest sense of failure. He was so furious that it drove him mad. How could he have failed so dismally? He was no novice or amateur to let himself be turned into a laughing-stock. He was no junior figure on this annual trek; he had spent a long time preparing for it and even longer waiting. More than anyone else he had to convince himself that he was a cut above the rest and had the ultimate power to get exactly what he was after. The others looked at him with a mixture of admiration and envy. To them this hunting trip was a measure of the way his hunting skills had developed during the course of an entire year. This was all the more so since this particular year had proved to be a full one; there had been various trips, all manner of false claims, and a collection of odd skills which many people had kept trying.

Whenever strangers arrive, this new test can be both real and irksome, the more so when they are outright amateurs. Their expressions are a balanced blend of admiration and doubt; at times they can show a good deal of fear, defiance and even contempt. A single word spoken out of place can kill more effectively than a bullet! Did he get any sleep that night? Did he dream about that huge mountain goat which would fall with his very first shot? Should he stick to that miserable rule which he had established, one which would apply to other people rather than himself: the goat, that's what I want?

Something happened that night.

As far as hunters are concerned, sleep is not just a much needed rest. It makes one hunter successful and another a failure. It can make one hand twitch and another be as steady as a rock. In his dream he saw himself standing on a whole mound of goats. There he was, with his foot placed nonchalantly on the horns of the huge goat which was leading the herd; he was addressing the novice hunter whom he had chosen as his companion and lookout in a clipped, contemptuous tone. He was looking at the others with a kind of modest pride!

Something happened that night.

He was waiting for dawn to break, but it never came. The other men were still asleep. He walked past the three cars and checked on that. The silence in the desert was so powerful and pervasive that it inspired a sense of fear and communion with some entity or other. When he woke his companion up, he had to wait for ages, long enough to smoke a number of cigarettes. By this time it was past three o'clock.

If he moved off now, he could reach the spot where he had twice missed the goat the day before. The going was rough, so much so that the car had refused to respond. For its part the goat had stood there in the distance and stared at him defiantly. That had been more than his pride could take; it was a case of utter contempt.

The pre-dawn twilight, yesterday's spot, the rough terrain, anger, defiance, sharp observation which can see everything at the moment of inception, and then once again anger!

As the darkness began to dissipate, the car's lights were turned off. Just before the sun aroused itself from its birthplace, a gleaming light emerged from somewhere; it gave everything an incandescent glow, and the whole scene looked brighter.

Using a cunning nurtured by hatred he made a big circle. He was anxious to reach the same spot just as the light came up and before the sun actually rose. He knew these places like the back of his hand. He would track that blasted goat just as surely as darkness falls in winter.

As it became gradually lighter, the horizon expanded. And then, in the bright, gleaming sunlight, he spotted the goat. It looked just like a point of light or the palm of a hand. It was the very same goat that had defied him the day before.

The rough terrain served as a barrier to both of them; it allowed him to move around freely, and his prey to run away and hide. In the cold, dusky, invigorating, brilliant light of dawn he spotted it between two rocks. This time he was ready, waiting for it with a hankering which was almost a passion. All thought about shots to the head and sides were forgotten; he was only interested in revenge. This was one of those rare moments. He slowed the car, turned the engine off, and slid quietly out. It was quite close now. He walked away from the car; as he moved forward, his heart was pounding. For a moment he had his doubts: was it the goat or just a rock after all; had it used some fiendish trick to vanish into thin air? He moved further forward; it was no more than thirty metres away now, just the distance he needed, wanted so badly.

He could stand it no longer; the goat's sheer defiance was more than he could stand. He had to teach it a lesson it would never forget. He would test his mettle to himself first before doing so in front of the others.

It does not matter whether it was the brightness of the morning light which enabled him to see that far, or if the shot hit the animal in the head or the left side. At such a range hatred becomes concentrated; the very lack of distance only serves to amplify the feeling. His anger reached its peak. In the bright light of dawn, the shot rang out. Its echo boomed, screaming, burning, deadly. He heard a tiny scream and saw the goat topple over a little. At that moment he was sure he had won. A feeling of sheer pleasure overwhelmed him, almost as though he were catching on fire. He wanted there to be dozens of people by his side to see how skilful, subtle and effective a hunter he really was. A single shot in the first light of dawn; it had obviously found its mark. If it had not been either in the head or the left side, the goat would not have toppled over like that, nor so fast.

As he walked over to the spot, he felt completely calm; in fact he was delighted and full of *joie de vivre*. Sleep, dreams, and thousands of utter falsehoods, he told himself, they're all the delusions of cowards and failures.

He moved further and further forward. By now the whole of creation was gleaming in the sun. There was a brilliant whiteness to the sunlight, and everything was so clear that the entire scene gave an impression akin to the crude immediacy of touch.

One more step, and he was there. His gleaming eyes were riveted on the goat's horns. There was the tiny kid with its head and a small part of its body already out. He watched the mother staggering over to the left but still doing her best to thrust the newborn creature out into the light of the world; she wanted to be rid of it before she died. As the goat looked at her offspring, her eyes were filled with tears!

The inhabitants of the quarter close by the Agha's garden had never seen or heard of anything like it. The whole affair was really remarkable. The bitch in the garden kept getting into the strangest sort of scrap, and twice a day at that. The first time was in the morning and the second just before sunset. At first people who had not witnessed the scene for themselves but had only heard about it from others refused to believe it; to them it was obviously some temporary phenomenon, something too weird to be repeated. But when they witnessed it for themselves, they joined everyone else watching the goings-on with increasing interest. Once they found out when things would happen and how it started and finished, the whole affair turned into something extremely exciting and managed to stimulate all sorts of contradictory comments. Most people explained this feud between the bitch and the two crows as being something as old as the hills and completely natural. To others it was simply a ploy on the crows' part to break the sheer monotony of their life and indulge in a particular kind of sport.

The way the whole thing got started is as close as you can get to sheer fantasy. Some of the people who witnessed the occasion reported that the two crows were flying from tree to tree in a thoroughly clumsy fashion, when suddenly the bitch started barking at them. Before anyone realized what was happening, the whole incredible battle started. One crow would fly in from the front, swoop down and brush by the bitch which would try to leap up at it. No sooner had this happened than the other crow would come in from behind and peck the bitch in the neck. When she turned round, the first crow would come in again from the front and peck it in the head or the back of the neck.

Eye-witnesses assumed that the whole thing would end in bloodshed as one of the adversaries finished off the other. Some people surmised that the bitch would get one of the crows by the neck and tear it to pieces, and then the whole thing would be over. However the game continued and even expanded. An element of sheer skill began to enter into aspects of the scenario which no one had even imagined. The reason was that the two crows maintained a safe distance between themselves and the bitch, and they did it with such finesse that the bitch was forced on many occasions to bark or pivot around quickly so as not to fall victim to their tricks. The crows kept pouncing in this subtle and conniving way, but they were never in a hurry. They would perch on branches on either side of the dog and wait for a suitable moment. The bitch meanwhile would be spinning around and barking like a maniac. But when she got tired and settled down into a particular position, the whole game would start all over again.

This was the way the whole episode started. The very same abruptness characterized its finish, and that was a disappointment to all concerned. But then the whole thing began a second cycle and almost always on time at that: first thing in the morning and at sunset. This provoked a good deal of astonishment and surprise. Some inner urge started drawing visitors to the scene. Those who at first were attracted by the strangeness of it all soon divided up into two camps, each one supporting one of the two adversaries and willing it either to finish off the other or at least inflict a genuine defeat. For that reason they gave the dog a name, Marjana. They could not do the same for the two crows because it was impossible to tell them apart; so they named them the Raiders.

The pattern of life in the neighbourhood of the Agha's garden is such that few people had the opportunity to follow this continuing conflict in the early morning. However, on spring afternoons the place would be crowded. Everyone in the neighbourhood was anxious to witness the battle and to see how the whole thing would end. In the late afternoon children would start taking up positions and betting with each other. Nursing mothers would bring their children and pots of tea. The men would come last of all. Every afternoon just before sunset, in a place which rarely changed, the battle would start. Cheers would be heard and boos too. One of the men might yell 'Raiders!' That would be a cue for the children to start yelling and screaming. No sooner did the crows pounce than the cry would go up: 'Marjana!' The bitch did not need any warnings; she was standing there poised and ready. At certain moments she would pretend not to hear or see. But, no sooner did she hear the sound of one of the crows swooping close to the ground nearby than she would make a demonic leap. However, in spite of all the force and momentum, the crow would glide back up to a place safely out of range. When the fun started, the children would be yelling, the men waiting in anticipation and the women acting scared. Everyone was expecting something to happen! Every sunset would bring an end to the game, but it would be craftily done, just like showbusiness! One of the two adversaries would pretend that they had lost the game and that the whole thing would restart in the near future.

The battle continued for the whole of early spring, and everyone enjoyed it thoroughly. It's true that, as time went by, the men became less interested and stopped getting involved as much, but the children did not let a single day go by without checking on the situation.

Then one day the whole thing came to an end. The bitch disappeared. No one saw the crows any more either. Some old people pointed out that, when the warm season comes, crows usually go to more humid spots; these two must have followed suit. 'Crows always do that,' they added confidently. Other men pointed out that human beings never know how animals are going to behave; their comings and goings and play habits are a complete mystery. Still others offered the explanation that the bitch must have got tired of the game: the crows' pecking had given her sores, while their constant cawing had got on her nerves; she could not stand it any more. The children decided to visit some of the other gardens in the neighbourhood; after all, a game like this one could never really come to an end.

That, at least, is what people had to say. The image of Marjana began to vanish from people's minds. When anyone saw a crow, they felt sure it could not possibly be one of the two they had seen in the Agha's garden.

However, in early summer some children spotted Marjana. The good news soon spread around the quarter. They felt so happy because they were convinced that the good times they had had before were about to be repeated. They started craning their necks to the tops of trees and the roofs of houses, looking for the crows. But none of the children noticed Marjana's expanding stomach nor her heavily-laden teats. A couple of days later, the children witnessed a strange sight: there was

Marjana with five pups behind her. The tiny, pointed shapes of the pups aroused a number of emotions in the children: love, admiration, and even uncertainty. Where had these pups come from? When the news was passed on to the older people, they nodded their heads knowingly and gave the impression they understood everything!

A short time later the crows returned. The children's delight knew no bounds, but the older people were somewhat more reserved and surveyed the whole scene with some circumspection. They thought about life and death, about trees and birds. However they too expected to see Marjana at any moment, a Marjana who was now both more confident and timorous. Around her pups she behaved with a haughty pride, barking loudly at anyone who came too close. She kept her head up to keep an eye on the crows, but otherwise paid no attention to their cawing as they flew from one tree to another. For their part, the crows kept their distance and stared at both Marjana and her pups and at the human beings who were watching the whole scene. And that was all they did!

The waiting became harder and harder. Those who did not enjoy watching the battles in the late afternoon found themselves unconsciously but resolutely waking up early, walking past the Agha's garden and waiting for a while, just in case something happened. They all pretended they were waiting to see Marjana and her pups. Sometimes they would even make wagers on the pups. Without even getting close enough to see, they would bet on how many were male and how many were female and even about which ones would be strong and which weak. Of course, there was something else behind all these wagers: they wondered when the fighting would start again and how the crows would deal with this veritable platoon of dogs.

And then without any forewarning, an air of tranquillity descended once again on the Agha's garden, just like the first time when Marjana and the crows had disappeared. The old people, men and women, were the first to lose their enthusiasm. Only the youngsters were left.

One June day which started off fresh and bright but which gradually grew hotter and hotter, seven shots were heard. The youngsters said later that the town policeman shot the dogs. Marjana was killed first. Even though he shot her in the side, he fired again just to make sure and then shot the five pups as well. Next day the garbage cart took the corpses of the six dogs away. The crows hovered over the cart and kept making a harsh squawking noise. People say that the donkey pulling the cart panicked, and the whole thing tipped over. They also say that the two crows kept on squawking and trailing the cart for the whole day. What is known for sure is that they were never seen in the Agha's garden again!

THE FOURTH STORY

On the day he arrived it was boiling hot. He had come from somewhere far away; they had covered hundreds of kilometres for him to get there.

For a long while he huddled in the corner, not following the lead of the other males who were showing off their speckled brown and white feathers. What set him apart from the other birds were his legs: they looked heavy and pointless. A lot of people were of the opinion that the amount spent on him was money down the drain.

How can men be so stupid? How can they cover such huge distances, all for the sake of something so futile?

These questions and many others like them were doing the rounds in the village. However he had come to an odd decision: one day something was going to happen. He had no idea what it would be or how it would come about, but he felt sufficiently confident to refuse to respond to any questions about the price he had paid for the bird or to talk about its capabilities. Previously he had been prepared to talk to anyone and at great length. As a result, the festival which the village usually put on during the early days of spring had allowed people to exercise their imaginations to the full. They tried to picture the shape of bird that would come and the skills which it would show in its performance. The bird owners from neighbouring villages were genuinely afraid, even though the wager was clear and unambiguous: 'That bird cost the equivalent of a whole year's produce. If he can collect more than a female or two, then pigeon-raising is all over for me!'

The bird stayed in the corner for a long time. First came regret, soon followed by bitterness. The sense of betrayal was overwhelming. 'Pigeon-raisers and hunters, neither of them can appreciate the full extent of destiny's reach.'

How can all this have happened?

One day he preened his feathers. Another day he moved out of the corner and sat in the warm spring sunshine. On still a third day he gave a coo and went slightly crazy while pacing around the big cage. When he decided to leave the cage and fly around, people were really afraid he was going to fly away and go back to the place he had come from, or that he would be a prey for other pigeons. He flew off and came back in a single day. His flight pattern was short and jerky, so much so that it made many people laugh and confirmed the very worst suspicions which they had kept to themselves. The other male birds were prancing around in the sun, longing to be released to take to the air; it was almost as though they could sense some hidden challenge. The female birds managed to maintain a posture of quiet relish at the whole thing and communicated silently with their mates. They too looked with interest at the newcomer. All this gave additional momentum to the sense of challenge which the other male birds felt. But for some innate caution which they all felt, a whole series of things might have happened.

Late in April something did happen. While no one could have predicted it, people did have some vague inkling of what might occur. It was something like water running or gusts of wind: the senses can pick up such things, even though there is nothing immediately visible to bring it to your attention. The bird suddenly sprang to his feet more vigorously than ever before and started cooing with a vengeance. The way he started strutting around inside the big cage signalled the beginning of a long struggle. This sudden development did not remain a secret for long. Soon everyone in the village learned that the cock inside the bird had come to life; he had decided to start the big game itself.

From that point until just recently no conversation has started or finished without some talk about the way he struts around and collects females like seeds, and that crafty aura of power which lets him lead flocks of pigeons as though toying with them or frolicking in the wind. Terms of admiration are to be heard as people look up at the bird cartwheeling in the sky above them.

These new statements of wonder played a sweet melody in his ears, and the expressions on people's faces provided an unspoken confirmation of his intuitions. He had more power now, and could do things which no one else could. The initial wager was followed by a second, and then by others. There was never any question of losing or reneguing. It would always get there; it might arrive late, but it always got there eventually. People who regarded the bird from this practical point of view and admired his prowess refused to picture him as just any bird. They wanted a real cock bird. However, he refused to be anything other than himself, pure and simple. People would feel particularly bad when they noticed him skulking in the corner with that tiny female pigeon.

'How can he stand that scrawny-looking female?' they would scoff. 'If he was a real bird, he'd be choosing one and more of the good-looking birds who are up to his standard. Then the offspring would be more powerful than father and mother together. He's as crazy as so many other birds.'

But she was the one he wanted, that quiet, sweet little bird with serenity in her gaze. Even though her body was large, she looked small and compliant. She would only ever give him anything after he had really worn himself out and was panting.

Inside those crazy veins of his something was going on.

The people who admired his way of walking and flying and who employed no end of hyperbole in depicting his abilities, refused to accept his life-style. In the afternoon young people would expect him to do wonderful things in addition to his strutting walk and clever way of flying. They used to talk about him very loudly so as to attract the girls' attention. They wanted him to behave like a real stud, the way some animals and birds do, so that they could laugh and talk even louder. That would be even more effective in attracting the girls. But the bird refused to cooperate. He strutted and flew just as they wanted, but continued to live the way he wanted. Meanwhile, the older people admired the bird's power and cunning. They found nothing about his way of life peculiar. To them it was all very natural, as though they were watching themselves!

He managed to produce one group of chicks after another, and they all learned a great deal from him. Then came the day when the village changed its name to Dovecote because pigeons from other villages kept leaving them to come to this village. This even applied to the crafty wild blue which people always used to talk about with some bitterness. It was incredibly difficult to get hold of; it lived in deep wellshafts and inaccessible caves high up on the rocks where it would lay its eggs. But even these species came in droves, one after another, and all via these new generations of birds.

As the days went inexorably by, stones would be washed away from high up on the mountains, leaves would fall from the trees, and people would lose their sense of tranquillity. Time had the same effect on the birds. The bird would walk around in the hot sun and survey a large number of other birds mingling in a multi-coloured patchwork of species. He would feel himself gripped by a single desire: to go on flying for ever and remain suspended between earth and sky. He was unwilling to abandon his habits, his flying or his way of life.

One day (in early spring once again) he got the feeling that his powers were present in a superabundance he had never experienced before. He felt that he wanted to fly far away; and he wanted her to come with him. He preened his feathers, walked around her and cooed. He told her the sky was the only place he could envision her as queen. When she refused to fly, he whispered in her ear that he could not stay on the ground; he had to fly. He strutted around with all the pomp, self-confidence and power of a king and then took off.

He made several turns in the sky and looked towards the ground. All around him flocks were swarming around rapturously. It was one of those moments when he felt he had everything. When he returned, he landed heavily on the roof. He wanted her to be waiting for him there, to gaze into his eyes and discover the distant horizons he had reached and the amazing things he had seen. But she was not there. He rested for a while and then went to look for her. She was in the corner, the very same corner he had used at first. There she was. He went over to her, looked at her quizzically and then turned away. He walked round her, but she looked the other way. He did it again and pushed some seeds towards her. She gave him a sad look and then turned away again. When darkness came, a cool breeze came with it. He moved in close to her to keep her warm, and she nestled up to him. She made an effort to go to sleep under his wing and to be at one with him. As he became drowsy, a cold wind started to blow. He felt he was close to her and united with her. They both fell asleep.

Next morning he could not believe it. He walked all around her and cooed to her more than ever before. He sprang up and exercised his claws and beak. He beat his wings against the walls. When the cage door was opened, the morning breezes brought an invigorating warmth with them. Everything seemed to be brimming over with life, and yet she remained still. He walked round her, and then again, but she remained cold. A little while later, she started to become stiff and dry.

All the flocks, small birds and large, started going out, but she stayed where she was. People came, looked sorrowfully at her and then removed her from the cage. He followed them to the end of the cage. Looking into their eyes he saw a silent confirmation of his worst fears. With that he staggered back into the self-same corner.

Three days later they removed him from the same corner. He felt dry too. As his body was tossed away, feathers fell from his crest and legs.

THE FIFTH STORY

No one can say with any certainty where he actually came from. Some people claim he was a wolf cub; others maintain he came from the mountains far away. Still others suggest that he was an ordinary dog with no distinguishing features, just like any other dog. To back up this assertion they would observe that his bark was just like a wolf's. When he was not barking and curled up in a corner, people would say: 'He's tricky; you never know when he's going to go berserk.' People will always spend a lot of time arguing about his origins and distinguishing features, but they always end up coining the same old phrase: 'The dog's the son of a bitch, and that's all there is to it!'

From the very first the dog moved about a lot and was easily excited. No one could ever work out how his floppy ears ever managed to prick up straight on top of his head like a couple of thick horns. As soon as he heard a noise, however far away it might be, his ears would prick up in a most amazing way. He was a little cross-eyed, and his eyes were forever watering, so much so that, if you took a careful look at him, his eye-trouble might seem to prevent him from seeing properly. One shepherd even went so far as to call him blind and say that he was useless. Another said that he had a hunting dog's nose.

He grew quickly and became much larger than those who had seen him as a pup expected. He often went crazy; no one could ever work out when or why. The Shaykh who had chosen the dog as his companion in this vast wilderness often had his doubts about the animal. Why had he selected this particular one out of the six puppies in the litter? What made him think he was the best, the one which would suit him the most? As he had looked at the pups and turned them all over one by one, something deep down had spoken to him. He had chosen this particular one; not the biggest or nicest to look at, but something had made him decide to choose him over the others.

At first he did not give the dog a name. Just three days later he lopped off most of the tail to make him look more vicious, an idea he had picked up from the villagers' talk. It took much longer to train the dog to stay with him and follow his instructions!

At a relatively late stage he was called Viper, a name which seemed almost to sneak in unnoticed. All previous names by which he had been called – Stumptail, Gray, Old One-eye, Imp – gradually receded, and this one stuck. The whole thing may well have been prompted by that confounded crawling movement which kept him some distance ahead of the sheep but in a position from which he could keep his eye on all of them.

The life and behaviour of dogs are both odd enough to prompt a number of major and significant questions in people's minds! They take a long time to form habits, but, once they have done so, those habits become so ingrained into the dog's mind that they become almost instinctive. Once Viper was eight months old, the other dog the Shaykh owned (which was two years older than him) became insignificant. Viper seemed larger and more powerful and alert. He gave the appearance of being in charge of everything and not relying on anyone else.

The dog would sleep by the paddock gate. He chose the spot for himself; no one did it for him. Every day before dawn broke, he used to go through a whole series of incredibly funny limbering-up exercises. He would crawl on his stomach for a substantial distance, using his splayed legs like powerful oars to pull himself along with swift strokes. After these manoeuvres he would go round and round in crazy circles, as though chasing his own tail. Every time he saw his truncated tail disappearing, he would speed up his gyrations as if he were about to catch it at any moment.

The Shaykh was very attached to the animal. That is why he was completely convinced that the dog was both capable and important. He stuck to his opinion in the face of the derisory guffaws which would greet this whirling performance. What started off as whispers eventually came out into the open as clear and explicit conversation: people suggested that, when the Shaykh grew really old and incidents of sheep theft and loss started getting worse, the owner of the flock would dispense with his services.

With the passage of time the life which the Shaykh and Viper spend together has assumed a particular quality of its own, something which is rare with two individuals even when they are both human beings. They converse and understand each other with the minimum of gestures. Somehow they seem instinctively aware of when to start a journey and when to end it. On cold winter days before it starts raining and nature goes mad as it changes its skin, Viper will surpass the Shaykh himself in his ability to comprehend the mysteries of the universe, especially since the Shaykh suffers from congestion, which worsens as he grows older.

The Shaykh seemed to grow more self-confident and even more youthful in a way, so he became reluctant to talk about Viper. However with the passage of time, the other shepherds who kept track of him and watched his movements noticed that the dog had some unique traits which no other guard dogs had. He moved around very little and was very quiet. Such was his determination that, just by looking at dilatory sheep in a certain way or driving them on, he managed to instil fear and dread into them. But it was only on rare occasions that he had to behave like that. Most guard dogs are trained to stay either to one side or behind a flock of sheep so that they can keep an eye on them or keep them moving. Viper on the other hand preferred to be out in front and on some high spot relatively far away. At first, the Shaykh was worried by this technique. It made him very wary of this blasted hound he had acquired because the dog would sometimes go further away than the Shaykh could see or tolerate. More than once this whole behaviour made him think about getting rid of the dog. After all, sheep are usually scared of noise, hand gestures and vicious dogs who nip at their legs or flanks to make them keep moving. But here was Viper positioning himself a long way away from the flock with that supercilious look of his. It became so bad that the Shaykh shot at him with his catapult and knocked his eye out. But life has many lessons to teach. Not many months passed before Viper took over everything. The Shaykh slept or wandered off into his daydreams; as long as Viper was around, he would often forget that he was a shepherd with a flock of sheep to look after!

There are no end of stories about Viper's cunning, energy and capabilities. The stories shepherds told were a blend of envy and admiration. Some of these would talk about the trips Viper took in aeroplanes to bring back new flocks of sheep from far away; they would be the cue for sarcastic jokes. Hardly had a group gathered together before the questions would come pouring out.

'Which one's ridden in an aeroplane more,' someone would ask craftily, 'Viper or the Shaykh?'

'Can the Mukhtar afford the price of a plane ticket, or will they be taking him with Viper?'

'With Viper riding planes all the time, is it so surprising if he goes crazy and acts so proud?'

As the days rolled by, a life-style of almost unalloyed delight prevailed over the village and gave it a particular stamp. But then something happened.

One day Viper vanished. The Shaykh spent ages looking for him; he searched all over the place and asked everyone. He expected him to return in the evening. He thought someone might have stolen or killed him. But he found not the slightest trace. Even so he did not despair for a single moment; he was sure he would eventually find him..

On the third day, Viper was discovered caught in one of the waterholes frequented by sheep. The Shaykh had no idea of how he came to think of looking there, but, once he thought of it, he was certain that was where he would find the dog.

Even before dawn arrived the Shaykh was to be found there trying to get his dog out. The animal was up to his neck in water with only his head showing. His eyes were inflamed, and his tongue was hanging out. He looked half dead. The Shaykh tried his very hardest to get the dog out of the water, but all his efforts ended in failure. No sooner had he almost got the animal out than he would fall back in again and sink up to his neck. With it would come all the despair of defeat.

That very afternoon the Shaykh's efforts came to an end and so did the dog. Only two days later the village walked silently behind the Shaykh's bier.

THE SIXTH STORY

This story will be found in *The Book of Animals* by Al-Jahiz. Several sources, among them Abu 'Ubayda the grammarian, Abu al-Qaftan Suhaym ibn Hafs and Abu al-Hasan al-Mada'ini, retell tales which they got from Muhammad ibn Hafs and Muslama ibn Ma'rib. This story was well known to the scholarly community in Basra. A virulent plague struck down the people in a particular house. Everyone in the district was convinced that no one, old or young, would have any chance of survival. A little boy in the house had been seen standing up and then collapsing, totally unable to remain on his feet. So all the other people threatened by the plague went to the house and blocked off the door.

Several months later, some beneficiaries under the will of the members of that household came by and opened up the door. When they reached the inner courtyard, they found a little boy playing with the pups of a dog which had belonged to the household. This was all very surprising. A few moments later, the dog which had belonged to the household came out. When the boy spotted her, he crawled over to her. The bitch offered him her teats, and the child started nursing. Everyone was fully aware that, when the boy had been forgotten and left in the house, he must have become very hungry indeed. Seeing the puppies making full use of her teats, he had crawled over to her. She had taken pity on the child and allowed him to nurse too. Having done it once, she had let him do it again, and he had availed himself of the food she offered. The sheer instinct which had taught him to suck his thumb immediately after birth when he did not know how to nurse had on this occasion given him the idea of nursing from the teats of the bitch. This instinct of thumb sucking and nursing from teats was not something acquired. When his hunger intensified and circumstances became desperate, it was sheer instinct and ingrained knowledge which led him to go over to the bitch and ask to nurse. All praise be to God who gave him the inspiration and directed his path!

THE SEVENTH STORY

What caused this enmity between him and mankind? When did it start? Why are there so many stories told about the bad luck he brings wherever he goes?

I will not deny that his walk is provocative, in fact almost arrogant. Nor can I deny that he loves to poke around in garbage cans for hours on end; he may even spend his entire life there. His voice may sound ugly at first, but it soon gets to be like that of most other birds. Needless to say, it is not more beautiful than theirs, but it is not uglier either. In any case sound and shape are inventions and ideas fostered by human beings to apply to animals for one reason or other. Who can say?!

This much is well known. But some people have gone so far as to suggest that the bird tends to pilfer and will make off with anything and everything it sets its eye on and can carry away, whether useful or not. Now that is a subject of prolonged debate. Some people have a whole host of stories to tell on the subject. Others will listen to such stories with a sympathetic smile and attribute the hyperbole which characterizes them all to a certain enmity between the bird and human beings, especially those who own walnut trees. The bird has a particular passion for walnuts and prefers them over any other kind of food. But then, every bird has a favourite type of food which they prefer to any other; they cannot be blamed for that!

He always maintains the stipulated safety-barrier between people and himself. It is not measured in terms of metres and paces, but has its own particular yardstick which varies from one human being to another. For peasants it is just a few metres most of the time. But when it comes to hunters, the distance is so great that only those who have experienced it can have any idea. Even though his flesh is inedible, two contradictory notions have become embedded in the minds of hunters. Some of them hardly set eyes on him before everything seems to turn grim, and they start feeling an imminent sense of disappointment; they may even end up blaming the bird for causing some failure they may have had on that particular day. Others can hardly get within range before taking shots in a thoroughly devious way; so many rounds get fired at crows that it is quite impossible to count them all.

One day I decided to spend the whole afternoon observing a pair of crows which had built a nest in a walnut tree at the end of the garden of the house next to the one in which I was living. This sort of pastime does not usually appeal to people, and indeed it would probably not have appealed to me if I had not been feeling thoroughly aggravated at the time. I had just heard that a man who lived in our quarter had burned his wife to death. The entire story left many people with a lingering feeling of sorrow. It was not just for the woman who had died, but because she had left six children to be looked after; the eldest of them was a girl no more than ten years old. As people told it, the whole thing was a matter predestined by fate, but that did not stop a rumour doing the rounds to the effect that the woman had burned herself to death because she could no longer stand the awful life she had to lead.

Every time I recall the tale, I am filled with a feeling of intense sorrow. I did not know the family, and in any case this tragedy was by no means the worst that happened in the big city. Every day would witness dozens of such incidents: suicides, murders and assaults, and heaven knows how many other catastrophes. But even so, the whole thing affected me deeply.

If that had been the end of it, the whole thing could have been forgotten fairly quickly, as happens with dozens of other incidents. But within two months the husband had remarried. His new wife made it a condition of their getting married that he should get rid of the children. The youngest of them was no more than four months old, but even so, he agreed to the condition without the slightest hesitation and married her. The news of his marriage spread even faster than that of the death of his former wife. When it comes to providing details of where the children went and how he dealt with them, people have different stories to tell. Some people maintain that he beat them all, even the baby, for a solid week; his idea was to make them run away and find somewhere else in the big city to live. Others say that he let the children starve for two whole days and that the baby died. It had been almost dead when it was moved to a neighbour's house. They had cared for it as best they could, but it did not survive. Still others said that, when a number of people told the former wife's relatives that they had heard the children crying, they came and took the children away.

The husband was asked about the children after he had married. People say that he looked grief-stricken and almost burst into tears. He assured people that his former wife's relatives had come and stolen the children while he was away and that he could not bear to remain alive for a single day with such an empty house. It was that, he said, which had forced him to get married again; he was afraid of going crazy or committing suicide!

It was either this incident or some other one perhaps which

made me feel so intensely sad. At siesta time on that hot August day I broke my usual habit and did not take a nap. I sat silently by the low window which looked out on the garden and watched what was going on. I must confess that it was this pair of crows that managed to attract my attention and take my mind off everything else going on around me. They were obviously preoccupied with something and did not stay still for a single moment. To cut a long story short, I witnessed something quite incredible: two crows were fighting over some walnuts with a stubbornness bordering on sheer insanity. If one of them managed to get hold of one, the other would shell it with infinite patience and perseverance. When he had finished, up he would fly and circle around. At first I thought he was taking it up to the nest, but then I changed my position and sat in a corner from which I could see the walnut tree itself and follow the game through to its end. I noticed the crow moving further and further away till he reached the edge of the next-door roof. From that great height he dropped the walnut to the ground. It smashed to pieces, whereupon he proceeded to pick them all up one by one and carry them up to the nest again. If they did not smash open, he would pick them up again and repeat the whole operation from square one; he might have to do the whole thing a number of times before the walnut shell would break open. At one point I saw the two birds picking up a number of walnut shells and pushing them towards a corner of the garden by the wall. When I say that they selected the most difficult and carefully concealed spots, I am not exaggerating in any way.

I found the entire spectacle very enjoyable. It took my mind off my own sorrows. I learned that a number of bird species have a high degree of intelligence!

What happened next was even more remarkable. Apparently the owner of the garden was fed up with these crows; he had made up his mind to get rid of them at sunset by destroying their nest. If he succeeded, the crows would leave the garden and find somewhere else to live. He may have been planning the whole thing for some time. The fact that he chose that particular time of day, tied himself to the tree with a rope, and put a short, sturdy stick in his waistband, all tend to confirm that he had thought about the whole thing and made some preparations.

The nest was high up in the walnut tree. In fact, getting at it was so difficult that the two crows who were hovering around the tree and surveying the nest were confident enough to regard this foray with a good deal of scorn. They were convinced that the nest was sufficiently high up and impregnable that no human being could possibly reach it. The peasant meanwhile kept on climbing resolutely and manipulating the rope in a clever and confident manner. Slowly but surely he inched his way up.

All the while the crows kept swooping down and then flying back up again in their usual arrogant manner. They dive-bombed the man and then soared upwards in a movement which combined contempt and warning. Before long however they became aware that the danger was getting ever closer and that the man was nothing if not persistent. With that they began flying in narrower circles and their cries began to assume a harsher, minatory tone. The man had a wiry frame and was a skilled climber. All the time he was getting closer and closer to the nest.

I sat there in silence, totally involved in what was going on. At first I felt completely neutral about the whole thing. The many stories I had heard about crows prompted within me a certain caution and lack of respect towards them; I might even express it as contempt. The man climbed ever higher, the crows' circles became narrower, and evening scents flitted on the breeze. I now began to realize that something of note was bound to occur. What would happen, I wondered, if the man fell or a branch of the walnut tree bent and snapped under his weight; perhaps all the shaking would dislodge the nest, and the chicks would fall to the ground.

As darkness fell softly and imperceptibly, the man was still climbing the tree. The crows had by now acknowledged this unforeseen threat and were screaming and circling at high speed. The chicks in the nest started screaming for help. Things were getting really serious now.

It was during these moments packed with tension and fear and so completely divorced from the usual dimensions of time

that something incredible did start to happen. Vicious screaming sounds could now be heard. One of the crows was circling
around the man's head, poised for attack and flapping its wings
loudly. He then flew back and perched on the nest. Now the
other bird began to fly to and fro from the nest to the man's
head; the movement looked just like a stone tied to a piece of
thread swinging back and forth. As the man climbed slowly but
relentlessly up the tree, the circle grew smaller and smaller.
The man was totally determined, and climbed cautiously but
resolutely. By now the chicks were in total panic, and their
cries took on a different tone. The crows themselves had gone
completely berserk. The tension increased with every new
stage in the unfolding drama.

Words cannot possibly describe the final moments. As the
man got close to the nest – one step, a mere hand's stretch,
away – the whole world went mad; everything became a blur.
The chicks were now shrieking in sheer terror, and the large
crow could no longer stay serenely in the nest. The other bird
stopped gyrating and launched a new line of attack, divebomb-
ing the man directly from above, attacking him with its wings
and entire body, and pecking and scratching him all over. The
man divided his attention between climbing the tree and
warding off these attacks. And then, almost like the onset of
darkness, the whole thing came to an end. The crow pounced
and managed to gouge the man's eye out; quite how no one will
ever know. But the man's determination stayed with him. He
grabbed hold of his short, stout stick and swung it. Two cries
were heard, one from the man, the other from the crow as it fell
under the force of the blow. Next day the female crow moved
the nest somewhere else. On that very same day she could be
seen in the corner of the garden using her claws to pick up
walnut seeds among the thorns and carry them away, one at a
time, to some other place.

THE EIGHTH STORY

In March an oppressive hot spell arrived, bringing with it all
the smells of the soil. Nature fanned out. Some early flowers

came into blossom. Small, reddish leaves appeared on the trees in all their early profusion, adding a serenity to the scene which already exuded a sense of sheer languor.

Two old men wrapped in goat-hair cloaks were staring out of the big window at the vista of the garden spread out below them.

'It's going to be a hot summer this year,' one of them said. 'The hot spell in March has come earlier than usual.'

'Hot weather in March is tricky,' the other replied with a rasping voice.

'We normally get another cold spell after March,' the first one went on. 'But this time it looks as though summer's arrived for good; we won't be getting any more winter.'

'Haven't you ever heard the proverb which goes: Keep your biggest logs for March?'

'But you can see how hot it is now!'

'In previous years we've had lots of hot days, but they were followed by cold spells and floods. We've even had snow in April.'

'Nature seems to have changed its rotation. When we were young, it was cold all winter. We would still be shovelling snow off the doorsteps in April.'

'That's all over and done with now.'

'True enough, but who knows ...'

The two men carried on this way. It was almost as though they felt they had to make small talk with each other. Nothing seemed to rouse their interest or enthusiasm; even the warmth which from time to time made itself felt seemed part of the normal routine. The only break occurred when the servant came in with some coffee.

'God grant you good health, Salim,' the guest said. He paused for a moment. 'You've done just the right thing,' he continued in a different tone of voice. 'If it weren't for you, things would be very difficult.'

The servant mumbled something inaudible and made a few gestures which managed to convey at one and the same time a sense of humility and sadness. The two men carried on watching life through the pane of glass. They looked at the trees, the flowers and the gentle breeze toying with the lush greenery of the leaves as they burst into bloom. They both wandered off into the world of distant memories, recalling any number of events from the past.

Down in the garden two sparrows were flying around in wonderfully symmetrical patterns. As they soared and swooped, their almost devilish expertise made all this frolicking seem like sheer madness. Here was such a display of skill that the birds' antics could not remain an undisclosed secret. The two men had almost nothing to say to each other, and so they found themselves drawn almost automatically to the antics of these two sparrows. The two men watched the birds' movements through the window, exchanging glances without saying a word. All the ideas and phrases which were taking shape in their minds receded into the background. Wonderful things were happening right before their eyes. The sparrows carried on with their non-stop performance; it was as though they wanted to be at one with nature, with the entire universe; to shout at the tops of their voices, and to tell the whole world how wonderful this warmth felt and how beautiful was life as well!

The servant had sat down on the outside balcony and was watching from a distance. From time to time he cast an eye in the direction of the two men. He felt the urge to pursue something which he could feel without knowing what it really was. He had no ideas or words of his own, but he still had the feeling that everything around him was bursting out and shouting; it felt almost as though there might be an earthquake at any moment. The two men were still watching as the birds cavorted their way through the sky. The servant kept flaring his nostrils in relish; he longed to strip off his clothes and feel a sense of unification with something, with nature itself.

'Salim,' yelled the owner of the house to rid himself of the feeling that he was being watched, 'bring us some more coffee.'

Salim got up forcefully from where he was sitting, made some more coffee and brought it over slowly to the men.

'If it weren't for you, Salim,' the guest said, 'the world would be a dismal place.'

Salim shook his head bashfully.

'Salim's all-important to us,' the guest told his friend. 'Even those people to whom we've paid money to do the job properly haven't done a thing!'

Salim withdrew quietly to the outer hall.

Nature in all its lavish effusion filled the entire world with its own particular aroma. At every moment trees seemed transformed in a headlong rush. The two sparrows kept up their wonderful routine and continued the entertainment. It was at this moment that it happened. Salim cannot for the life of him remember exactly how it all came about. Somehow the two birds were flying about in the same crazy, carefree formation, as though they were involved in some kind of reckless race or else had a bet on with each other. The moment was fraught with inexpressible significance. As quick as a flash one of the birds assumed that it could penetrate absolutely anything. Careering down like a meteor in quest of new horizons it crashed into the clear, gleaming pane of glass, through which the two men were watching the scene, and fell to the ground.

'See how deadly love can be!' one of the men said as he watched the bird on the ground.

'Yes indeed!' replied the other, 'just see how lethal it can be!'

The bird had such a feeling of rapturous agony when it landed on the ground that it felt almost like laughing or making love. It kept rolling over and over as though it were ravishing everything in sight. The other bird thought at first that the whole thing was no more than one big crazy joke, but, as soon as it realized that something was afoot, it began to get worried.

Everything had happened so fast that it all seemed like fantasy. The other bird circled, landed and waited, then walked over to the first bird, stretched out its beak and prodded its companion. The bird on the ground was turning over and over like a swatted fly; it looked terrified and hopeless. Within moments its movements began to dwindle and then stopped altogether.

'Just look what passion can do,' the first man said.

'As you said,' the other man replied with a loud laugh, 'see how love can kill!'

Salim was listening to them talk. He got up slowly and went

over to see whether the bird was still alive or dead. The tiny body was still warm as it lay there in his hand, but life had gone out of it. The bird shook its body once more, but life had already left. Salim remembered the old days and especially the Sunday of the week before.

'Did you pray over her in the big mosque?' the guest asked his children anxiously. 'Who walked at the head of the procession?' he asked once he had assured himself of their answer to the first question. 'How did people look? How good was the chanter? Who are the people buried beside her? Did anyone I don't know come? Did the whole thing take a long time?'

The man was sitting in the middle of the room to receive people's condolences. He looked sad but resolute, and seemed completely alert as well. He enquired about all the people who came; he had even more questions about the people who did not come. From time to time he would repeat in a firm voice: 'When your turn comes...'

Salim remembered it all now. No sooner had he picked up the bird to throw it over the wall than he heard another loud crash. When he turned round, it was to see another bird fall in exactly the same spot. He looked anxiously. The scene was the same, and the very same images flashed before his eyes. But he was never able to decide whether it was the second bird which had decided to emulate the first or that two new birds had started playing the same game with the same result!

THE NINTH STORY

In Al-Jahiz's *Book of Animals* we read:

There is a species of rat which loves playing around with coins, gauze, *dirhams* and trinkets that make a jingling sound. Sometimes it brings them out of its hole and starts playing with them and all around them. Then it puts them back one by one until they are all in place again. Al-Sharqi ibn al-Qatami tells the story of a man from Syria who was watching a rat take a *dinar* out of its hole. When he saw that the creature had taken some real money out, greed got the better of him. He was just about to grab the money when he changed his mind; prudence brought him to his senses.

'I'll wait until it has stopped taking everything out,' he thought. 'As soon as it starts putting any money back in the hole, I'll pounce on it and grab the money.'

And that is precisely what the Syrian did. He went back to the place from which he had been observing the rat. It brought out all kinds of stuff and then started putting one piece of money back in. When the rat came back for another piece and discovered that it was not there, it started jumping up in the air and crashing to the ground until it died.

This is the kind of tale which women and people like that will tell you.

THE TENTH STORY

Rex was a little dog as white as snow. He had hair like a tiny lamb's; it was soft and curly and hung down over his eyes. All you could see of them were two narrow slits which blended in with the rest of his face. His most distinguishing feature however was the thin snout which came to an abrupt point in a reddish-brown patch, a combination of hues which is rarely found in such an attractive combination!

Rex spent most of his time indoors; he was only rarely allowed outside and then only with someone. This exercise was part of the small village's daily routine. No sooner had he emerged from the house in the Major's company than he became the cynosure of all eyes and the major topic of conversation. They would talk about the way he behaved, how he raised his head to look at the faces of people staring at him, and how he raised his leg to relieve himself. But the thing which amazed everyone the most was the obedience which the Major could command from the dog. No sooner did he give that short sharp command than the dog would feel a moment of panic and stop whatever he happened to be doing. If the Major told him to come back or to stop barking, there would not be a moment's hesitation.

This relationship and other factors coloured the way in which the villagers thought of the Major. They regarded him with a mixture of fear and admiration, with a measure of mystification thrown in as well. Even owners of hunting dogs were perplexed by such obedient behaviour and secretly longed to be able to train their dogs as well. It made them think back to all the stupid things their hunting dogs had done over the years, things that had made them forfeit a lot of guaranteed game!

People had dozens of questions to ask, but there was only one occasion on which they were prepared to ask them: that was when the Major's batman was in charge of the dog. Some people would make a point of showing their admiration for the dog; they would do so in a loud voice and would try to ingratiate themselves or else walk alongside the dog for a long stretch. At appropriate points they would ask their questions: how had the Major managed to train the dog so well? Where did the dog sleep? What did it eat? Did it understand anyone else's commands besides the Major's? Sometimes the Major's batman would be in a good mood, and then he would answer whichever questions he felt like answering. By so doing he would amplify the process of mystification still further and shroud the whole situation in even more fantasy, all this by way of showing off the dog's unique intelligence. He would tell them how the Major had long conversations with the dog and so did the Major's wife. The batman admitted that, while he himself could understand some of the dog's clever actions and behaviour, there were many other things he could not fathom at all! This applied most of all to the large amount of time he would spend in the Major's wife's bedroom; he noticed that that would be the cause of many unfathomable problems!

Now the Major was a prominent personage, both awesome and inscrutable; and he had unprecedented powers. The military forces he commanded controlled everything, not just in the village but in many other areas as well. These troops had a special camp at the edge of the village. Among his visitors would be prominent figures from the village or guests who would come there on urgent business connected with security, border issues and other matters. The Major would always have Rex with him when he met these people, and he would often interrupt the conversation in which he was involved to talk to Rex or else to scold or threaten him in some appropriate way.

People even said that on more than one occasion the Major took out his pistol to threaten the dog. On such occasions he would use the local dialect which he had managed to learn. The words and threatening expressions he used in that dialect were often interpreted in more than one way!

The villagers, rich and poor alike, used to regard the Major and his dog in a very particular way. The poor people would sneak looks at the two of them as they were sitting in the tiny cafe and recall the numerous stories they had heard about them. The pup and the wolf, they would say. Then they would pretend to be busy doing something else so that they would not have to copy what the rich people always felt bound to do, namely stand up respectfully and greet the Major. It did not matter whether he was in his shorts and carrying a small ball in his hand to train the dog with or wearing his elegant white dress-uniform; he would always be striding along arrogantly without paying the slightest attention to these greetings and bowings. In fact, he would often ignore them completely, pretending instead to be deep in thought or else talking to the dog.

When certain things happened in the village, everyone, rich and poor alike, would act scared. Anger and inspection would spare no one. At the very last moment, when the investigation and general onslaught were at an end, the Major would take a delight in bringing Rex with him. The dog would wander around wherever he liked with complete freedom. He regarded everything as a plaything, and thought nothing of licking people's faces, well aware that they could not stop him or resist in any way. Everyone wished that the Major would look at them the same way he did at Rex.

Stories about the village, the Major and Rex went the rounds for a long time. Probably no one really wants to tell the whole story, but there is a part of it which the entire village will always remember.

One late afternoon on a cold winter's day, the sky was already getting dark. At this particular time of year, the packs of dogs which had been born and had grown up in the village since time immemorial used to stick together in groups. This sort of system had its own special rules, something which every dog knew by instinct and never infringed in any way. Somehow Rex managed to get among them; to this day, no one knows how. He was alone, without the Major or his batman, and was thus unprotected and undistinguished in any way. A wretched bitch was lying there in the middle of a circle which all the dogs respected and maintained with an amazing regimen. What happened on that winter day after sunset was all simply confirmation of the rules of the game. The powerful dogs, the seasoned campaigners, were taking advantage of priority rights, and all the other dogs knew that none of them could interfere or break the code. However exactly the opposite happened. Rex appeared and caught everyone's attention. The rich people started behaving in their usual fashion. The dogs on the other hand did not notice him or pay the slightest attention. They could have made room for him inside the circle, but in fact something very different happened. Rex barged his way into the circle like an idiot. Everyone just sat there thunderstruck. The dogs looked at each other and then at him. In the flash of an eye (or actually before that could even happen) one of the dogs pounced on him and ripped most of his back wide open. In a trice Rex fell to the ground with a howl of agony, giving some pathetic whimpers for help. The other dogs meanwhile continued their fun under their own particular rules.

What ensued simply falls under the category of daily details. The Major ordered all the dogs to be killed; that much is true. For that purpose he drafted a number of soldiers in the regular army. But before long another Rex appeared. This time, the dog was from one of the larger dog species. People had different opinions as to what the dog's role was: some maintained he was a guard dog; others that he was supposed to follow in the other dog's footsteps; still others that this dog was strong, and could kill and lord it over all the other dogs. The Major's batman had some cryptic things to say which no one could explain.

'The Major's wife chose him,' he told them. 'It's her dog, not the Major's.'

The village dog community started to grow again and continued to bark both before and after the Major's departure. The new Rex was killed in obscure circumstances. No one knows who killed him or why!

It was a cold winter's day. As usual on Thursday, I decided to warm up some water for a bath, that being a private whim which I have indulged for a very long time. It reminds me of many things: my youth, days long ago when as a young man I would go with a group of my friends to the market baths. It also reminds me of certain smells to which, for some obscure reason, I am particularly sensitive!

I had kept up this ritual for a very long time, but it had only assumed its full significance when I started doing everything for myself: chopping wood, drying it, collecting the kindling and making a pyramid-shaped pile so that the fire would catch quickly. Once this phase was completed, I would select a number of medium-sized branches, space them out in a criss-cross pattern and mount them so that the wind could whistle through and speed up the fire. The final phase consisted of my placing big heavy pieces of firewood on the top. Once the fire started to blaze, I would feel confident about everything; I would test the warmth of the water before leaving my place behind the house for that favourite corner in the interior room from which I could look out on everything. Then I would lapse into a private reverie until the time came to take my bath!

I used to set about these rituals with relish. Two of my children use to stand there watching as I went through each move with an exquisite delicacy. I did however make every effort to appear as uninterested and nonchalant as possible. But just as the fire caught hold and the bluish-yellow flames started to flicker their way upwards, I heard a very disturbing noise.

'Those blasted creatures,' I yelled angrily. 'They build their nests in the worst places!'

I remembered how pigeons used to build their nests in chimneys. That in turn brought back the memory of the huge amount of effort I had expended a few weeks earlier to remove the remains of a nest from the chimney stack; all so that the smoke could make its way upwards unimpeded by such totally stupid blockages. In any case, I told myself, the few small branches and vines which are left from the nest cannot possibly keep the smoke from going up; they'll burn up, for sure. Taking a step backwards I looked up to make sure that the smoke was indeed going up. I saw a dark cloud making its way forcibly upwards, and felt greatly relieved. I was on the point of brushing off my hands before going back indoors and heading for that favourite corner of mine when I heard a noise even worse than before. I stopped and rubbed my hands together while I thought about the situation. Once again I looked upwards. The smoke was going straight up at first and then curling over as the wind caught hold of it. I told myself that a dry twig must have fallen from the top, while at another moment I had a visions of pigeons' eggs. But suddenly there came a suppressed but piercing noise. I took another step backwards and in an unconscious act of self-defence grabbed hold of the two children. Then I waited.

In an incredible, scream-filled moment I stared as a cat scared out of its wits came tearing out of the fire. It was really frightening. I shuddered and shut my eyes. When I opened them again and took in the scene, I could not believe my own eyes. It had taken me some time to get the wood ready and light it. As the twigs had caught fire, my lungs had choked on the smoke, and I had been forced to move back. I had kept rubbing my eyes with the back of my hands to wipe away the tears which kept coming. By the time the large branches had caught fire, this had been going on for some time. As I reconsidered these moments and asked myself in amazement what could have happened, I realized that the cat must have been paralysed with fear; otherwise it would surely have got out and run away.

'The way that cat stayed in there was amazing,' I yelled as I rubbed by hands together to keep them warm. 'The smoke alone was enough to choke it. How can it have stood the heat from the fire?'

I took a step backwards to see what had happened to the cat. What I saw was horrifying. Most of the animal's skin was burned; its whiskers and much of its face had been completely charred. It looked almost comic.

The cat spent a few moments recovering its breath and licking parts of its burned body, but then I saw it shake itself and stand up. I assumed it would go somewhere and hide to take care of itself and suffer through its pain out of sight of prying eyes. But instead it charged towards the fire even more recklessly than before, obviously bent on breaking through so as to get back to where it had been before. It seemed totally oblivious to the fire and smoke and to the fact that the three of us were standing watching. In an unconscious gesture I grabbed a large piece of firewood and tried to use it to block the cat's way. But it responded by hissing and spitting angrily as it dodged the outstretched log and tried to plunge headlong into the fire. For my part I made an even greater effort to stop it, and the cruel game went on for quite a while. Every time my vicious thrusts managed to keep the cat away, the animal became more defiant and determined than ever to get through the fire. And eventually it did just that.

Much later we were drinking tea as usual and watching the news on television.

'Do all cats behave that way?' asked one of my children who had watched the whole thing.

I gave him a long stare and noticed how sad he looked. 'Cats aren't the only ones who behave that way,' I replied. 'All animals do.'

Silence followed. Any number of thoughts were going round in my head, and I was on the point of saying several things. For the most part, I felt bitter and angry. 'Human beings should learn that bit of information very well,' I whispered.

'What's that you said?' my son asked me with a quizzical look.

'Nothing, nothing,' was my only response.

Once again there was silence. I raised my hand to scratch my head, hoping to get rid of both the dirt from the fire and the miserable thoughts I was contemplating. I wanted to behave in a way which would allow me to rid myself of a life in exile!

THE TWELFTH STORY

Hunters differ widely on the subject of rooks and whether or not you can eat their flesh. Some maintain that rooks belong to the crow species; as long as crows peck at corpses and live in garbage dumps, they are not worth looking at, let alone shooting. Others will tell you that rooks are migratory birds who only eat the very best seeds and drink the sweetest spring-water; as a result their flesh is juicy and tasty, certainly not something to be compared with crows'. They may be similar in outward appearance, but their feeding places are completely different. And, in any case, it is one's own senses which should govern what can and cannot be eaten.

When hunters start arguing, this subject comes up so often that they quickly change the subject and start discussing other types of bird! But deep down they all have a secret craving to find out more about this particular species. The two – crows and rooks – look very much alike, in their size, the noise they make, and the way they fly. The big difference between them is the rook's jet-black colouring, like the darkest of dark nights. Furthermore rooks fly in large flocks. During the winter season they can normally be seen on their daily flight in the early morning and just before sunset.

Hunters usually steered clear of rooks, either because of the bad luck they were supposed to bring or because their flesh was tough. Often they would look up at the black flocks of rooks as they flew back in the early morning or else on cold spring evenings; their expressions would show a mixture of malice and frustration. When other birds were in scarce supply and their frustrations got the better of them, they would look even more resentful. On such occasions all the stupidity lurking inside a man inevitably turns into an accursed demon which starts careering off in every imaginable direction.

Some hunters choose swallows as their target, but those birds have traversed the entire world in order to get back to their nesting place and so they do not offer themselves easily. No sooner do they dart across the sky with that furious flapping sound than they will dart off in another direction, almost as though the bird comes to an abrupt halt or remembers its mate or its nest and feels bound to go back. As they zoom off in different directions, all the shots fired at them by hunters go wide of the mark. At that, the hunters get really furious, and the sky erupts in a pandemonium of wild shooting. Through all the blue smoke and smell of gunshot the swallows simply dodge the bullets, continue on their way with massive contempt, and eventually reach their nests.

Situations like this can drive people mad; they finish up looking almost like dogs frothing at the mouth. Even hunters, who will always put on a big show of being detached and who are well aware of what can and cannot be eaten, get bitten by the bug. When it gets really dark, they start substituting bats for swallows. Shots start being fired with the same reckless abandon, and things stay that way till the hyena start howling and the pitch dark of night shrouds everything. All this arouses in man an instinctive fear of everything around him.

On one such occasion three hunters had failed to catch anything and were feeling utterly frustrated. They had completely exhausted themselves over a period of many hours and wasted innumerable shots; the ground was littered with cartridges. A little before sunset the flock of rooks were returning from their daily journey. As they swarmed in an almost circular formation in the sky and came slowly towards the hunters, the sight of them was both exciting and provocative. The men sat there spaced apart, smoking and ruminating on their failures. The flock circled in the sky. The swooping and soaring of the birds produced a muffled sound, but it still managed to cover a broad swathe of territory. The men looked up resentfully.

'Just crows,' one of the hunters told himself.

'Too high to shoot at,' said another.

'If I can't land myself one or two of them,' said the third, 'they can cut off my head and crucify me!'

The flocks kept moving confidently and proudly on their way. The three men, their minds full of racing and clashing ideas, followed the birds' spectacular progress, each one from his own spot. Just then one of the hunters fired.

The flocks of birds gave a start and immediately the air was filled with their squawking, a sound which totally drowned out the noise of the shot itself. At this point one of the birds faltered. It lost its equilibrium and started soaring and gliding; it was making a determined effort to continue flying. It flew high above the other birds in the flock, and then from even higher it plunged to the ground with a terrible screech.

The hunter who had fired the shot looked overjoyed as he

rushed to pick up the bird. It was a long way, more than two hundred metres. He felt happier with every step he took; he was set on recovering his prize. At first the birds had been devastated by the unexpected attack, but, with every step and gesture the hunter took, they began to draw together into a pack. Shrill squawks made their way earthwards or hovered close to the ground around the fallen bird. As the hunter approached and the bird stopped moving, the whole atmosphere became electric.

The hunters began to make their way back. You could see the traces of blood on the man's face, hands and right ear, all in the gleam of the headlights of cars going in the opposite direction. There was complete silence. Only when the three hunters got back to the city and the light from the headlights filled the entire car, was the silence finally broken.

'God curse those blasted birds!' the hunter sitting in the front seat said. 'They're not even worth the cost of the shot!'

'This time I was really scared,' said the driver, stopping abruptly. 'I was afraid none of us would make it back alive.'

'I told you, they're not edible,' the first speaker went on. 'They're crows. And, even if they were edible, they bring bad luck!'

The third hunter remained silent. His face, hands and ear were all aching badly. At one point he was aware that he had stomach ache too and felt like vomiting!

THE THIRTEENTH STORY

Even when he laughed, his eyes had a cruel expression. When he decided to scold or be sarcastic, you felt really scared, but, more than that, your basic instinct was to run away. Such an expression would certainly imply the possibility of reprisal even in the very best of circumstances. When the Bey was in a good mood, you could still expect a string of words to emerge at some point, sounding more like a curse than anything else. Everyone was afraid of him. People talked a great deal about the unusual cruel streak which was his hallmark, something which set him apart from all the other rich people in the district and others as well!

When he drove in his black car, children would run away; when he rode by on horseback to make a tour of inspection of the acreage he owned, they would do the same. The way older people had become accustomed to doing all kinds of obeisance to him was close to serfdom; it involved standing up whenever his car went by or he rode past on horseback. Some people who were more fortunate and powerful even went so far as to enquire after his health and mood. No one could strike up a conversation if the Bey did not initiate things. 'Oh, the Bey's feeling out of sorts,' they would say, or 'The Bey has lots of problems and doesn't want people to distract him.'

They had other things to say as well: about his many business interests in the capital, his enemies who would be ruined because of their attitude towards him, and the larger number of responsibilities waiting for him!

When he was on his estate, everything changed: his expression, his behaviour, even the weather. So many tales have been told about him that he has become a sort of legend in his own right ...

Once in a while he would bring a number of friends out to his estate. No one ever knew with any certainty what went on behind the high walls of the big mansion, but everyone was aware it was something momentous.

The people living on the estate say that the Bey owns a large collection of hunting weapons and equipment. They claim they have never seen him use the same gun twice. His skill as a hunter has become so famous and proverbial that they would note that the Bey only scores hits in the flesh; all of which proves that he never misses his target!

Hunting days would change along with the seasons, and so would the friends who accompanied him on these trips. No one in the village can ever remember a guest hunter returning with more game than the Bey himself. This is the way he would deal with the game: certain parts of the catch he would keep as a token of his skill and prowess, but the rest he would leave for others, especially people who came from the capital. He always insisted on keeping some rather peculiar items: heads of large goats, pelts of strong and rare animals, and occasionally birds which no one else hunted! The servants living on the estate confirm that there are a large number of goats' heads around, too many to be counted. These servants prefer not to talk about a lot that goes on in the mansion. However they would occasionally reveal one or two details, and that only added to the general obscurity surrounding what went on: the Bey's life, the number of guns, the number of goats' heads and animal pelts, and other things as well!

On hunting days the entire village would be transformed. People used to look out for the caravan's return; they would be keen to find out what they had brought back, where they had gone and when they got back. In fact some people were so curious that they would get up at the crack of dawn and watch through their windows or from the rooftops as the procession of cars left. They would notice how it moved, at what time, and how many cars there were; they would certainly observe that the Bey's car was leading the way ... and so on.

One day a strange-looking truck arrived in the village. It was green and looked like the ones which are used to transport vegetables and fruit. But this one was brand new. Mounted in the middle of the carrying space was a plush chair, the kind used by barbers; it could swivel all the way round and shone in the sunlight. It was firmly mounted to the floor of the truck. The arrival of this truck aroused a lot of interest. No one could guess how or why this vehicle was going to be used. The servants on the estate seemed to have had some advance notice and to know something about it, but even they could not provide any answer to this new question. They supposed the Bey must be planning some novelty for the estate, something which would cause a big stir! Two days later, the Bey himself arrived with a group of friends.

Young children did not usually participate in the hunting trips, but they still talked about them a lot. They would make up any number of stories and never tired of retelling them. Something really amazing happened on this particular trip. The Bey asked for two children to go with him on the green truck and help him. I have no idea how it happened, but I came to be chosen. It was the first time I had ever been out hunting. I had gone with my uncle on short trips, it is true, and had enjoyed them very much. On one occasion I had even tried to persuade him to let me take a shot. But he told me that he had so little powder and shells with him that there was only enough for three shots. At that I stopped asking. I decided to grow up quickly so that I could do what grown-ups did.

Before the trip started they mounted a machine-gun on the green truck. The Bey watched as the operation proceeded and supervised the whole thing himself. He was obviously very proud of it, although he had very little to say. There was the usual bustle all around him, but it was tinged with an uncanny calm, almost a premonition of what was to come.

At midnight a number of cars and guns were made ready. The procession was to head towards the Western desert. Because it was going to be a long and tiring ride, the Bey rode in a jeep while everyone else rode in similar cars. At the back was a large truck. The new green truck with its embellishment came second, right behind the Bey's own car. After a whole day's travelling the party reached the camping-grounds of a Bedouin shaykh. This all caused a big stir which completely disrupted the desert scenario, involving as it did songs, celebrations and feasting. We two youngsters were sitting in the rear of the green truck with our backs against the netting which covered the sides. The Bey gave us one of those never-changing looks of his, almost sadistic and calculating. We ate some of the things we had been given, and then the Bey's attendant told us we had to have the cartridge belts ready for the Bey. We had to pay close attention and have quick reactions as well because hunting required those qualities. The reason why the Bey had chosen us was that he needed two small excellent helpers who did not take up much room and would not get in the way of the chair as it swivelled around. His last words to us were that we should not get scared when the bullets started flying all around us, and we should not worry about the noise it made.

By now the Bey was in the chair. He was heavily-built and portly, and so above us we had a formidable pile of compressed flesh. The chair revolved impressively, making a swishing sound as it turned.

No words on earth can possibly describe the scene that ensued. As bullets flew all over the place, the whining sound created a terrifying extravaganza of noise in the open desert spaces. The gazelles charged hither and thither in every direction in a state of total panic; and that made the scene all the more horrifying. The Bey was shouting his head off at every salvo; he seemed almost drunk or crazy. Once in a while between salvos we managed to raise our heads and get a glimpse of the utterly unforgettable scene.

All the Bey was interested in was firing bullets – and plenty of them at that. The gazelles kept charging all over the place in utter panic. At times they would leap higher than the truck itself and then either collapse to the ground or else hobble around with their legs broken and their innards hanging out; the whole scene might have been almost comic. In this broad desert expanse these antics themselves had the impact of actual explosions!

'You're still young!' my father told me when we got back to the estate. 'You can't take it all.'

'The evil eye has struck me,' my mother said, 'and you've got to do something to drive it away.'

I cannot remember what happened to me after that, but my mother maintains that I died and then came back to life. No one knows how it happened because the fever I contracted is usually enough to finish off a fully-grown man.

I never saw the Bey again. Once I had recovered, my father sent me to the city. 'Village life is no good for someone with your skinny body,' he said. 'You must continue your schooling with your uncle in the capital.'

I never returned to the village. Any time I heard a single word on the subject of hunting, I would feel extremely morose. Whenever I set eyes on a gazelle, even if it was just a picture, I would start feeling feverish and sick.

Many years later, the Bey's corpse was found hanging in the main square. I do not know why it happened: whether it was because of the gazelles or the human beings whom he had killed.

Next afternoon I stumbled across a modest place to live. It was a long way out, almost a suburb. I did not bother arguing with the old woman about the terms involved. They were simple and straightforward. There were two categories of rent: one for rich tenants who would pay the complete amount requested; the other for the poor and needy, in which case the amount could be reduced by half provided that the tenant was willing to take the dog for two walks a day.

'As you can see,' she told me to soften the blow. 'I'm an old woman. I can't walk very far, nor as fast as Karuf likes to go.'

It only took me a moment's thought to agree.

The entire situation was at once exciting and worrying. How can anyone form a relationship with an elderly dog? And, as if that was not enough, this was the first time I had got to know a dog at all; I had always had a deep-seated contempt for dogs in general.

It took quite a while to train the dog; a number of walks were required to do it. Madness does not afflict humans alone: it can also affect animals. Karuf (that was the dog's name) was a case in point. On many occasions he would become stubborn and mean, and no amount of cajoling or threats would serve any purpose. If he was not brought out of it at once, he was capable of doing any number of stupid things!

On one of our joint walks when he was first undergoing training, he went absolutely berserk. We wore ourselves out trying to calm him down and placate him, but to no avail. Just then the old woman shouted 'Miro!' By some mysterious process the dog was transformed in a flash. He started looking around and sniffing the air. As he searched all over the place, he forgot all about his furious temper. In fact he had become a completely different dog.

The dog walked along obediently beside her without any chain or leash. 'If he gets like that again,' she said, 'all you have to do is to say "Miro".' She scratched the dog's back as he kept looking around and sniffing the air. 'But please,' she went on, 'don't do it unless it's absolutely necessary. It wears him out!' This magic password kept ringing in my ear, and I wondered how I was supposed to explain it. Every time I asked the old lady, her expression would become strange and sad, and she would change the subject. Then came the day when she told me. 'Miro's my husband,' she said without the slightest warning, 'my husband who died seven years ago. He used to look after Karuf and was very fond of him. Purely by chance, he was alone with Karuf when he died of a heart attack. I had gone out. I came home and realized that it was too late to do anything, but Karuf refused to believe that Miro was dead. When the priest and mourners arrived, he did all sorts of incredible things; and when they tried to take Miro's body away for burial, the dog caused a lot of problems.'

As she was telling me all this, her voice kept getting lower and more subdued. I saw tears trickling down her furrowed cheeks. She paused for a moment to recover herself. 'Karuf's still waiting for Miro to come back,' she went on. 'He's still waiting. He can't go to sleep without the smell of Miro's scent: it can be a piece of his clothing, one of his tools, anything of his. Whenever he goes berserk or feels miserable, there's only one way of getting him out of it, and that's to shout for Miro.'

Ever since then my life has seen a number of changes. The fact that particular things have happened may help explain that. Linda's love for me had its inexplicable aspects, and so did the way in which she left. I still cannot understand why she felt compelled to be so incredibly abrupt and cruel as to inform me after the very first time we slept together that she was never going to see me again. Quite by chance I bumped into the old lady and her daughter in the supermarket. I walked over to say hello and have a chat, but they simply walked past me with a glare of contempt, almost as though I were some disgusting vermin from another world.

That day I returned to my room to find Karuf waiting for me. As I put my key in the lock, he was scratching at the door. When I got in, he jumped on me lovingly. The old woman was standing in the corner gazing quizzically at the scene.

'That's what he used to do when he was waiting for Miro,' I heard her say slowly.

When Karuf heard the word 'Miro' he was delighted. He left me and headed for the door. There he stood waiting!

As these stories unfolded one after another, people were amazed; their curiosity aroused, they wanted to hear more. These tales were not told the way stories are usually told elsewhere and on other occasions. 'Assaf's corpse seemed to pervade the entire room, and his presence increased the effect. It created an aura of fear which permeated the whole assembly, although it took different forms. This fear posed such a challenge that, at least initially, no one felt able to leave or even move. But then one of the stories really shook up the Mukhtar. He got up abruptly. It was an almost unconscious gesture, like a sleep-walker or madman. With a nervous gesture he removed the covering from 'Assaf's face.

''Assaf,' he said defiantly, 'you were the one who knew all about animals and birds. You lived your life for al-Tiba. With just a few hours of sleep you would leave and head for the desert again. How can man be so barbaric and animals better than he?'

The Mukhtar's words were unequivocally clear, although tinged with sorrow. He paused and then turned his head a little. It looked as though he were putting his ear close to 'Assaf's mouth to catch the answer. There was a prolonged silence. The Mukhtar turned, put his hand on 'Assaf's shoulder and shook him gently as though waking him from sleep.

''Assaf, 'Assaf,' he said, 'did you hear what I said to you?'

Bitter condemnations were now heard from the men present. 'Don't be such a fool, man,' they said. 'Cover him up again and come over here. You're the Mukhtar; you're supposed to keep your head! 'Assaf's dead and gone. Don't be so stubborn; stop asking for the impossible!'

But the Mukhtar carried on in the same nervous tone, as though he had not heard a single word they had said. ''Assaf, 'Assaf, why don't you answer?'

The atmosphere in the room was heavy with the aroma of death. Normally people can be expected to use their common sense. However in circumstances like these, they certainly lose control and turn into some kind of herd being led by a madman. Harsh words had already been uttered. The Mukhtar now found himself grabbed under the armpits by powerful hands so that he could be lifted bodily back to his place. But even that did not prevent him from continuing this gruesome game. They picked him up forcibly. For a moment he just stood there, but then he collapsed, and they carried him back to his place. He had hardly got there before standing up with even more vigour than before and lunging towards 'Assaf once again.

'Now look!' one of the old men yelled at him. 'If you're going to carry on like this, we'll all leave you and go home. You know what happens when anyone is left alone with the dead: he either goes mad or else joins him in death!'

It was as though a thunderbolt had descended from heaven. The Mukhtar turned around suddenly. He pushed away all the hands which were enveloping him, curled his fingers together and moved his hand up and down to make them wait a moment. There was complete silence.

''Assaf must hear everything you say,' he told them in calm, measured tones. 'That's the only way he can be sure that the people of al-Tiba have either turned into human beings and deserve to stay alive, or else that they are still as stupid as they were before!'

He gave them no chance to respond. 'We must prop his back up,' he continued, so as to allow what he had just said to sink in. 'Then he can keep an eye on us and see who is telling the truth and who is lying.'

'We must show respect for the dead,' retorted one of the elders who by now was fed up with this fit of madness which seemed to have afflicted the Mukhtar. 'We should observe the proper respect to the very end. Using the dead for play-acting or fun and games like children is both an insult and an offence to our religion.'

The compromise to which they all eventually agreed was reached through a mixture of cunning, common sense and sheer bluntness. The Mukhtar was to return to his place. In return they would remove the covering from 'Assaf's face.

One of the guests felt as though his very stomach was going to leap out through his throat, but he summoned up the courage to speak. 'I hope the assembled company will forgive me,' he croaked nervously. 'We're responsible for everything that's happened. If it weren't for that ill-starred trip we took, none of this would have occurred.'

'Everyone's lifespan is in the hands of God, my son,' one of the elders intoned to crush all argument and change the atmosphere. 'When someone's final hour comes, there is no way of either advancing or delaying it!'

'This was the way 'Assaf wanted to die,' another man said. 'He kept saying in front of everyone that he wanted to die in the desert, on a hunt, with his dog by his side and his rifle either on his shoulder or in his hand!'

Some of the elders and more prudent people from al-Tiba tried to change the subject to some remote topic, but unconsciously and almost involuntarily the conversation kept reverting to the subject of hunting and birds and animals. Every time dogs and gazelles were mentioned, the Mukhtar would look over at 'Assaf.

'That's exactly what you used to say,' he would comment in a hurt tone. 'Listen to them! Now you've left us, they're saying exactly the same thing ...' He paused for a moment, and a sarcastic smile came over his face. ''Assaf's crazy, they used to say. 'Assaf's a loafer, he doesn't like work. Now here they all are repeating exactly the same words that you used to use!'

Whenever anyone in the company lost his temper with the Mukhtar or told him to keep quiet, he would nod reluctantly.

'Go ahead,' he would say. 'You can say whatever you like now.'

It was one of the most incredible nights in the whole of al-Tiba's history. The people of al-Tiba are normally tolerant, but there are occasions when bitter feelings will overwhelm their sensibilities and goad them into something close to anger. If anyone else had done what the Mukhtar did that night, things would not have come to a peaceable conclusion. But they all realized that the Mukhtar had been through a whole series of tragedies. He had lost his only remaining son during the last war. He had searched high and low between al-Tiba and the city to find out whether he was alive or dead. The officers in the city had had no words of comfort for him, merely repeating over and over again that he was 'missing in action'. Then his wife had died suddenly during one of his search trips which had lasted for several days. He had come back to al-Tiba to find his house empty. When he told people that God had taken His deposit, his attitude had at first seemed peculiar but later on it had become more stinging. This double disaster had affected the Mukhtar badly. He seemed to waver between sanity and madness, and at times his behaviour could seem very peculiar. As a result no one in al-Tiba was unduly surprised at the way he behaved that night, although no one had imagined that his mood could turn quite so bitter and defiant. Ever since his own personal tragedy, all he had managed to say over and over again was: 'I don't believe it. How can this have happened all at once?'

Al-Tiba knows how to treat people harshly and also how to deal with such behaviour from others. But it can also show extreme kindness and will never abandon any of its children. There was a slight suggestion that the Mukhtar's condition was so bad that he could not carry out his duties and that the Western segment of the area should be looking for a new Mukhtar. However the entire idea was greeted with both derision and outright rejection; it all came to nothing. Everyone was agreed: al-Tiba shows just one face, not two. It would never abandon any of its children even if they fell or lost their way. People in other villages and communities might behave that way, but al-Tiba certainly had never learned how and had no intention of doing so now!

The stories had had a particularly emotional effect on the Mukhtar himself, but no one remained unaffected. Everyone felt themselves overwhelmed by a surge of grief. And there was a whole host of questions to be answered. At several points everything had almost the same effect as an electric shock. What was the meaning of life and death? Why did creatures have to die in this devastating fashion? How would it be if man could live a more simple and honest life and rid himself of all his gadgets, things which had managed to turn him into a creature who only knows how to collect things and then destroy them? How is it that, during times of drought when people are starving, the city has nothing to say, but it will proceed to recall other times and seasons which are not even worth bothering about?

These and dozens of other similar questions kept buzzing through the minds of the people cloistered in that room. It was certainly spacious, which made it clear that at one time the Mukhtar had owned quite a lot. But now the whole thing looked very shabby and neglected. An all-pervasive layer of dust had become part of the scene. Furthermore everything looked disorderly and somewhat dirty. All this made people uneasy. There was a general desire to wrap things up as soon as possible. On top of it all, there lay 'Assaf, his expression frozen, his eyes dimmed, and a limp, sarcastic grin staring straight at them. Not even the most courageous and steadfast of the men present felt entirely secure.

An elder suggested they open the window facing South.

'Leave everything just as it is,' the Mukhtar yelled at him.

Was it the memories that were making him behave like this, or the sheer desire for confrontation? He seemed determined to proceed this way to the bitter end, even if it involved death.

Things can be explained any number of ways. Each answer may have its own particular validity and truth to it. Everyone in the room had been sucked into a whirlpool of grief, and so no one felt ready to defy the Mukhtar or go against his demand. All they could do in such circumstances was to play along with him and treat him like a child.

Along with all the stories and memories, grief and other sentiments now began to emerge. The Mukhtar kept making comments, many of which were sheer nonsense. And yet he still managed to stay in control of the proceedings and to give them his own particular stamp. Whenever a gazelle fell victim in one of the stories, he would yell out:

'That's precisely what 'Assaf used to say. Only once in his entire life did 'Assaf down a gazelle.'

He paused for a moment. 'Don't you all remember the way he used to talk about gazelles. I'll never forget the phrase he'd use: "Gazelles cry ... as they're dying, they always cry; it doesn't matter how they're dying, they always do it." That's why 'Assaf would never copy those greenhorn youngsters and other heartless types by hunting gazelle.'

When the topic turned to dogs or other animals, the Mukhtar would get all upset and start waving his head like a pendulum. If he had something to say, he would not hesitate for a single second.

This was the way the longest night in al-Tiba's history went by. For reasons which are both obscure and complex, the younger people were more tolerant of the Mukhtar's behaviour. One way or another the elders managed to keep their feelings on the matter to themselves. Finally dawn came. It was then that 'Amm Zaku who had built most of the houses in al-Tiba decided to change the topic and spoke up loudly.

'Do you all realize what has to be done?' he asked.

Everyone looked round at him. 'You honour the dead by burying them,' he went on in the same tone. ''Assaf must be buried at first light.'

It was with a great deal of skill that 'Amm Zaku now gestured to a group of young men to get up and go with him to prepare the grave. He himself stood up.

'Get him ready quickly,' he ordered. 'When the grave's ready, I'll send word for you to bring him!'

The Mukhtar had fixed ideas on how 'Assaf was to be buried, and there was no arguing with him. The elders tried discussing the whole thing, but he shook his head and gave a gesture with his left hand which made it abundantly clear that he would not listen to any further discussion.

'That's what the officers and soldiers told me,' he replied when they kept arguing. 'I asked them about my son and the other soldiers killed during the fighting. They're buried in their own clothes because they are bound to be much holier than all the linen the city can produce.' He was almost jocular as he went on: 'And as you all know full well, al-Tiba doesn't have enough linen to clothe the living. In a year such as this one, how is it supposed to clothe the dead?' He became serious again. ''Assaf's death was not natural. He died for al-Tiba; he's a martyr. He wanted to be this way while he was alive, and he would certainly not have wanted to change his appearance at the very end!'

Things were getting more complicated than anyone could have imagined. They gave in to the Mukhtar's wishes, although with not a little remorse. Everyone came to the forceful realization that, whatever happened, the whole thing should be concluded as soon as possible. If it were allowed to linger on, all kinds of complications might emerge; and then no one, sane or insane, would be able to come up with the right answers!

If this had been the most remarkable night that al-Tiba had ever witnessed, then the day that followed it was no less so. The sun was only a little way up in the sky when 'Amm Zaku sent a number of messengers to report that the grave was ready and that they should hurry. But the Mukhtar kept refusing to cooperate, treating them in a manner close to contempt. He insisted that the time was not right. After a lot of insistence 'Amm Zaku came himself. His technique required both nerves and cunning. In a loud and categorical voice he proceeded to issue instructions to the effect that no one should interfere with things about which they knew absolutely nothing.

'Listen, you people from al-Tiba!' the Mukhtar yelled, obviously overwhelmed by the whole thing. ''Assaf's no thief or highwayman to be hidden away and buried in the dark. He died for all of you. That being the case – and I saw it with my own eyes, he should be buried when the sun's high in the sky, at a time when all the people in al-Tiba will know about it!'

Everyone assured him that the people of al-Tiba were well aware of everything. They were all waiting for the moment when 'Assaf's body would be carried out so that they could join in his cortege.

'Let him see you all,' the Mukhtar said. 'He loves you all and wants to see and hear everything for himself!'

And so the moment arrived when 'Assaf was carried out. No one can say whether it was when the Mukhtar wanted it to be or whether other people prevailed. He was carried out of the guest-house on a bier, wrapped in a black cloth. All those who witnessed the spectacle confirm that he was not really carried, but rather that he flew. From one point to another he seemed to move through the air even faster than a bird. Everyone in al-Tiba came out to accompany the cortege. They all tried to find something to do. Those who could not help carry the coffin ran alongside, and those who could do neither tried to do something else. Since time immemorial al-Tiba had kept its guns in storage, and the older people had always talked about them with a great deal of pride. They loved to recount how they had got hold of them, how much they had paid, and what particular qualities the weapon had when they had used it in battle. Without any prearranged signal or prior agreement all these weapons were brought out for the occasion. Others sensed that they had made an error by coming without their weapons and immediately sent their children or relatives back to get their own. Within a short space of time al-Tiba had taken on a strange appearance very reminiscent of a certain point in the Great War some ten years earlier when they had faced the enemy and stopped their advance, losing a large number of men in the process.

As it wound its way from the Mukhtar's house to the graveyard, the procession was guided by unseeing hands and voices. The Mukhtar himself had three weapons which he used to protect his house, but he dispensed with all of them and chose instead to carry 'Assaf's old weapon. From time to time he loaded and fired it; it almost felt as though he were at a wedding. The sound of shooting filled the air. Even people who had only a few bullets to spare and were trying to save them for other occasions made up for it all by firing blindly into the air. There was an element of defiance to their shouts, but most of the time they had no particular significance; or rather they acquired significance by the way they blended in with the movements of people's hands as they carried the coffin. They kept moving it rapidly onwards, trying to make sure that it floated through the air and flew on its final journey…

For all this speed and skill the procession moved very slowly and arrived late at the South Hill. People had come up with the crazy thought of taking it down alleyways so narrow that people cannot pass each other. The idea seemed to be that 'Assaf should see everything in al-Tiba for one last time before leaving it for ever and vanishing beneath the earth. To the accompaniment of ululations, gunshots, a crazy stampede of people, and goodness knows what else, 'Assaf's cortege took a little over an hour to reach the place where he was to be buried.

Everyone was waiting at the graveyard at the beginning of the foothills to the South. No one can say how the crowds came to be there or where they had all come from. Some had come from villages close by and even from others further away. They had used some remarkable means of transport to get there:

huge buses and trucks. The children from neighbouring villages had come on donkeys and bicycles. They had all decided to wait there because no one in al-Tiba knew with any certainty where the funeral procession was at that particular point or where it was going. A dignitary from one of the neighbouring villages suggested that they should all gather by the graveyard; that is how this mass of people, machines and riding animals happened to be there. It was as if some huge magic hand had brought them all together in one place and then spread them out in such an incredible way.

No sooner had things quietened down and the procession started to climb the foothill slopes than people started to repeat the phrase 'There is no deity but God' over and over again. The shouts were accompanied by the same crush of people wanting to help carry the coffin, all of which caused a good deal of confusion. As new hands took hold of 'Assaf without any idea of the weight involved or the best way of carrying him, the coffin started a rapid semi-circular motion. Many people maintain that they saw it fly through the air and that no one could keep hold of it or even touch it. The distance from the slopes to the place where the grave had been dug was no more than two hundred metres, but it still took a long time to carry 'Assaf up there.

It is not just the men in al-Tiba who are known for their crazy ideas, their tolerance, affection, cruelty, defiance and temper. The women are the same way. No one can remember how it all happened even at the very end. 'Assaf's body had just reached the grave when the women of al-Tiba gave him a welcome befitting such a man. Nothing was made to seem special or unusual. Yet no sooner had the coffin arrived and been lowered to the ground in preparation for burial than the women gathered in a circle and started a rhythmic, orderly dance which blended elements of sadness, joy, pleasure, insanity and anger. The steps were complicated, and so only the women who were used to performing the dance could do them properly. They were accompanied by shouts, and that gave the whole performance an emphatic beat and allowed for a more subtle rendition. As the dance and shouting proceeded, the men continued their work with extreme care. 'Amm Zaku was still in charge of the whole thing. When he asked them to lift 'Assaf out of the coffin and to help him lower the body into the grave, the whole operation was handled with consummate skill. The men who were asked to carry out these duties showed a certain amount of confusion in their gestures, but soon recovered their customary poise. 'Assaf was placed in his grave, and 'Amm Zaku gestured to them to lower the long, thin slab of stone which was to be used as a covering, followed by another small stone which served to seal the hole. The corners and edges were taken care of, and the whole thing was finished off with great skill. The men carried out their task deftly; not a single word was uttered. The circle of women started to spin with even greater speed and intensity. Emotions reached such a pitch that at one point some women took off their head-coverings and others clutched their shawls as they began a kind of hysterical dance. Once in a while a sound would be heard which lent a fresh impact to a particular movement and made it seem all the more emotive.

None of the men objected or interfered while this was going on. It had only ever happened once before: that had been ten years earlier when some men had been killed by the foreign troops and they had been brought back to al-Tiba for burial. All that time ago, the village had done the same thing for those men. People still retained some of their Bedouin habits and hated to express their grief in this fashion, but, when their sorrow reached such a pitch that no one could stand it any more, then anything was permitted. Al-Tiba had witnessed its fair share of uncouthness, something that may well have reached unacceptable levels. At any rate it was not normal for the village to let its women go out to the graveyard to participate in burial ceremonies; it preferred instead to wash its hands of what was referred to as 'God's chosen charge' as quickly as possible. But the wishes of a few educated and well-balanced people could not serve as the only stimulus for everything al-Tiba did. There were many occasions when it would do whatever it thought necessary and it alone reckoned would save it from an even worse fate. So, when the men saw the women gathered together there like a black mass in the middle of the sloping hill, they were all overcome by a feeling of intense sorrow. They realized that 'Assaf was merely one of many men whom the village had buried. His death was obviously an event of great significance. Still no one could believe it had actually happened; nobody could bear to see him go so fast and in this particular way. Everyone participated in throwing in the last handfuls of earth, even the young children. Only the small group of women who were still spinning around deliriously and had no idea of what was going on around them did not get involved. Those handfuls of earth felt like dagger-thrusts aimed straight at the heart. There was complete silence.

With heavy footsteps people now began to tear themselves away. Each slithering pace down the hillside seemed to be dragged forcibly from the very earth itself. When the men reached the bottom and stood by the buses and trucks, the only thing that could be seen further up the hill was the figure of 'Amm Zaku with a shepherd alongside him clinging to his pan-pipes. 'Amm Zaku's expression was stern and sullen; he was staring off into the distance as though to garner a particular sound from the mountains and valleys of al-Tiba and the desert as well. The shepherd was standing there waiting, apparently starting some tune or other. Around the two of them stood some boys and a group of women. The group became gradually smaller with every passing minute as people became more and more exhausted and sank to the ground. Everyone moved nervously as though the whole thing were an act of vengeance. By now the women were totally worn out. One after another they buried their heads in the soil and burst into uncontrollable weeping and screaming. Both men and women of al-Tiba, it seemed, were weeping over its fate in a way they had never done before. Even so, there was anger mixed in with the weeping.

By now the Mukhtar had recovered his poise; at this point he seemed quite lucid. He suggested that a number of people should head straight for the city from the graveyard to discuss the question of the dam for one last time. No sooner had he spoken than the response was both bigger and better than anyone could have anticipated. The response was not restricted to people from al-Tiba either; many men from neighbouring villages expressed the desire to accompany them to the city. The men sent their children and relatives back to the village with their weapons. They gave clear instructions to carry them back carefully and clean them properly because they might be needed soon. That took just a few minutes. Then one after another, the cars set off for the city. There were large and small models; some of them were so old and worn out that they needed a push-start and a great deal of patience as well. As the procession went on its way, it looked like a peculiarly shaped piece of wire. Inside the cars the men said nothing. Once they had left al-Tiba, they stayed on the rough dirt track which led to the wide asphalt road. At that point most of them turned to look in the direction where the people from al-Tiba were pointing.

'That's the way to the place where the dam's going to be built,' they said.

The Mukhtar said almost nothing all the way, but at one point the person sitting next to him heard him say:

'I'm not going back to al-Tiba again, unless it's to carry a rifle and stay up in the mountains. Up there and with other people to help, we can do great things besides hunting. If they agree to have the dam built, I'll come back on top of a bulldozer and begin the job myself. Then al-Tiba will begin to appreciate the real meaning of life, instead of having to endure this living death it leads every single day.'

Once again silence reigned. All that could be heard was the sound of the cars on the asphalt road as they headed for the city.